A Single Virgin 2
AN UNHINGED ARRANGED MARRIAGE

KRYSTAL ARMSTEAD

A Single Virgin 2: An Unhinged Arranged Marriage

Copyright © 2025 by Krystal Armstead

All rights reserved.

Published in the United States of America.

All rights reserved. No part of this publication may be reproduced, distributed, or transmitted in any form or by any means, including photocopying, recording, or other electronic or mechanical methods, without the prior written permission of the publisher, except in the case of brief quotations embodied in critical reviews and certain other noncommercial uses permitted by copyright law. For permission requests, please contact: www.colehartsignature.com

This is a work of fiction. Names, characters, places, and incidents either are the products of the author's imagination or are used fictitiously. Any resemblance of actual persons, living or dead, businesses, companies, events, or locales is entirely coincidental. The publisher does not have any control and does not assume any responsibility for author or third-party websites or their content.

The unauthorized reproduction or distribution of this copyrighted work is a crime punishable by law. No part of the book may be scanned, uploaded to or downloaded from file sharing sites, or distributed in any other way via the Internet or any other means, electronic, or print, without the publisher's permission. Criminal copyright infringement, including infringement without monetary gain, is investigated by the FBI and is punishable by up to five years in federal prison and a fine of $250,000 (www.fbi.gov/ipr/).

This book is licensed for your personal enjoyment only. Thank you for respecting the author's work.

Published by Cole Hart Signature, LLC.

Mailing List

To stay up to date on new releases, plus get information on contests, sneak peeks, and more,

Go To The Website Below...

www.colehartsignature.com

CHAPTER 1
Lottie

That Friday after court

"Yes, hi, ummm, I need to make an appointment with Doctor Mason. I need her earliest available." My heart raced that day as I slipped into the backseat of Zailey's car that morning after court. My hands shook as I held my phone to my ear.

Bonnie waved goodbye to me as she walked over to her car. I wasn't really paying her any mind. It was Friday, and I already knew she was going straight to Kelsuis's place to pick an argument with him so he wouldn't go to the club that night. Silly ass rabbit.

"Doctor Mason actually has some available appointments this afternoon. Just had a cancellation. Can you be here at 2:30?" the receptionist asked, her voice vibrating against my eardrum. My anxiety amplified her voice. If I didn't calm down, I was going to have a fuckin panic attack in my sister's backseat.

"Look at that nigga." Whitney huffed, getting into the front driver's seat. "His ass couldn't wait for the final judgment." She clicked her teeth as we all watched Jaclyn's car dart out of the parking lot. "The nigga can't wait to put his dick in another bitch. Probably going to fuck her right now. The bitch been gone a month and a half. He's gonna fuck her through the floor when he finds her."

Ouuu, that bitch got on my nerves.

"Y-Yes, I can make it by 2:30."

I peeped the time on Zailey's console. It was 1:45 pm. That court proceeding seemed to go on forever that day. The judge made his ruling, granting Jacyn half of our assets. He wasn't even the family court judge, but he granted Jacyn joint custody of Joel, telling me to my face that he didn't want Jacyn having to go through the battle of trying to get his son. That he knew how bitter and petty some women could be after a divorce. I wanted to tell the muthafucka that his hairline was bitter and petty for being pushed back like that, but I remained quiet.

"Okay, Mrs. Devereaux, I have you down for 2:30 p.m. Can I help you with anything else?" the receptionist asked politely.

Can you help me get my husband back? I thought. "No, thank you." I hung up on her, throwing my phone onto the seat before letting out a deep, painful sigh. "Take me to Matthews, Zailey. The doctor has availability today."

Both of my sisters looked back at me before looking at each other. Neither of them said a word, but I already knew what they were thinking: that I should've gotten that second opinion before I just gave my husband away. Trying to control my fate backfired on me. I never thought Jacyn would fall for another woman. The entire time that we were together, his eyes never wandered. He catered to my every need. He loved me even when I was a bitch. And I never appreciated it until I saw him giving that same unconditional love to another bitch.

Sitting in the doctor's office that day was sending my anxiety even further through the roof. I was there to get a referral to a new oncologist. I needed a second opinion. Before we even started our appointments, my primary care doctor always sent me to the lab down the hallway for bloodwork and a urine sample. After I left the lab, I sat nervously on the doctor's table, clenching my hospital gown, my heart beating rapidly. My sisters were there as usual for moral support. And Bonnie was blowing up my phone, probably to tell me that Jacyn was at my place, finally grabbing his shit. Well, what was left of it after I burned a few things. Maybe more than a few things.

"Good afternoon, Mrs. Devereaux. How are you?" Doctor Mason smiled as she walked into the room to greet me. Her smile quickly faded when she saw the tears soaking into my cheeks. She quickly cleared her throat, asking my sisters how they were doing instead of asking me. "How are you ladies doing?"

Zailey sat in a chair alongside Whitley, leg shaking, anxiously tapping her Prada heels against the vinyl floor. "We've been asking this little white girl to get a second opinion for over a month. *That's* the reason we're here. *That's* how we feel, Doctor Mason."

Doctor Mason turned her attention from my sister back to me. I'm sure by the expression on my face, the doctor could tell that I was tired of everyone calling me white when clearly I wasn't. It may have been my imagination, but her facial expression seemed to change from understanding my frustration to questioning my ethnicity herself.

She cleared her throat when she saw me rolling my puffy eyes. "I've been trying to call you for over a month to schedule the surgery to remove the tumors in your spine."

"She didn't see a reason to have those removed if she was told she only had a few weeks to live," Whitley spoke up before I did.

Doctor Mason looked at me with a blank stare on her face. "'A few weeks to live'? Where are you getting this information?"

"What do you mean?" Whitley exclaimed. "Her oncologist!"

Doctor Mason turned in her stool toward her computer. After finding the screen she was looking for, she flipped through a few tabs until she found my scans. "Her scans show tumors in her spine. And small benign tumors in her breast, which have been causing the redness and inflammation."

My sisters sat there in silence. I wasn't sure how they felt, but I definitely felt my heart sink to the pit of my fuckin' stomach.

"C-can you repeat what you just said?" Zailey stuttered. She glanced at me sitting there in shock before looking back at the doctor, who sat calmly at her computer.

Doctor Mason pushed her Chanel glasses over the bridge of her pointy nose and turned the computer in our direction, so we could see the scans for ourselves. She pointed to the image of the tiny dots on my spine and the tumors in my breast. "All of these are operable. None of these are fatal. Your scans were clear of any malignant tumors. What second opinion were you searching for?"

I wanted to throw up. I could feel the air rising in my chest. If I had spoken up then, I would've either cried out loud, threw up all over that room, or both.

"Doctor Alex told her back in August, on the fuckin' 29th to be exact, that she had a short time to live because she had inflammatory breast cancer!" Whitley did start to cry for me. "How the fuck are you telling us that my sister is cancer-free when that other doctor told my sister that she was dying?"

Doctor Mason shrugged. "I have no idea how the doctor mixed up her scans, but the ones showing here in my system with Mrs. Devereaux's name—"

"Ms.," Zailey corrected her.

Doctor Mason frowned in confusion. "Excuse me?"

"Ms. Devereaux. Not Mrs. Devereaux. Her divorce was finalized this morning," Whitley snapped. "My sister—against our advice—filed for divorce from her husband to allow him to remarry to inherit her share in our family's group home because she was told that she was fuckin' dying! Now you're sitting here telling us that there's some other woman out there who's dying and probably doesn't know, and my sister is going to live? That her tumors are benign? That she didn't have to hand her husband over to her cousin?"

The doctor hesitated to speak as she watched me hold my stomach and jump off the table to run over to the nearest trash can. Everything I'd eaten that morning before court came spraying out into the trash can. The moment I was finished hurling in the trash, I cried out loud.

Zailey got up from her chair to rub my back while I coughed and threw up some more. "We're going to sue the fuck out of that doctor!" Zailey's voice was muffled as I dug my head further into the trash can to prevent chunks from flying onto the room's clean, sanitized floors.

"My team will reach out to the cancer center to alert them of their devastating mistake," the doctor said as if she didn't know what else to say. As if mistakes like that happened all the time.

"Devastating mistake?" I lifted my head from the trash, and Zailey rushed over to grab a paper towel for me to wipe my face. I snatched it from her to wipe my mouth. "I divorced my fuckin' husband over this!"

The doctor looked offended, like I was blaming her for the other doctor's mistake. "The oncologist made the mistake of mixing up your records with someone else's. The files were probably placed on her desk by her assistant, who is really the one responsible for the mistake. The results were definitely not yours. We can send you to another oncologist to confirm this. Though you were misinformed, no doctor would tell you to divorce your husband, the main person you would need by your side in a battle for your life. You made that decision on your own."

Zailey helped me stand from the floor, scoffing in disgust. "I don't think that's any of your unprofessional business." She helped me back over to the bed. "Your only business is scheduling my sister for another scan with a clinic that doesn't make these kinds of mistakes."

The doctor disagreed. "My business is to make sure that *Ms.* Devereaux gets the care she needs. If you want to get a second scan, I can get you squeezed in as a favor this afternoon with one of my colleagues who's an oncologist out in Concord. She can have your scans interpreted and entered in your Atrium App this afternoon as well. And while you're here, we can get you scheduled for your first OB-GYN appointment."

Whitley damn near snapped her neck looking over in the

doctor's direction. "What do you mean? Does she have cervical cancer? You just said she was cancer-free!"

The doctor rolled her eyes. She never liked it when I brought my sisters with me for moral support. I used to bring my mother. I needed support at the doctor's office because I was terrified of the news that I would get. I'd been in a battle with my own body for twenty-one years. A battle no one lived but me. But despite how alone I felt, I could always count on my sisters to take my health even more seriously than I did.

"Her urinalysis results show the presence of human chorionic gonadotropin, also known as hCG. The pregnancy hormone." The doctor watched Zailey and Whitley both turn to me, arms folded.

"You fucked that nigga the night you told him that it was over, didn't you?" Zailey hissed. My sister knew my fuckin' sex life better than me. She knew I wasn't fuckin' my husband on the regular. She always told me that she was surprised the nigga waited for me to divorce him to show interest in another woman. "*That's* why the nigga had no issue moving onto your cousin!"

"Well," the doctor got up from her stool, smoothing out her jacket, like she achieved her goal of pissing off my sisters, so the attention was turned back on me for divorcing my husband and off her colleague, who'd fucked up, "I'm going to reach out to my colleague to see what time you can come in. The technician will be in with the appointment time. She will also put in a referral to an OB-GYN. Then, you can head over to check out." She faked a smile before heading out of the room.

My sisters rolled their eyes at the doctor before looking back at me for answers.

"Scarlett, you just divorced this nigga!" Zailey's voice bounced off the walls of that cramped room and probably throughout the walls of the hospital, from how fucking loud she was yelling. "You left this nigga damn near everything you own in your will except the house our parents gave you! You know he's on his way to find that bitch to marry him!"

Whitley looked at our sister before looking at me, sitting there on that bed, thinking, plotting. "A baby, Lottie? You don't want a baby."

I nodded in agreement, getting up from the bed to go over and grab my clothes. "No, I don't, but Jacyn does."

The silence in the room was deafening.

"We've been telling you this entire time to get a fuckin' second opinion!" Zailey watched me get into my clothes. "Doctors fuck up all the time, misdiagnosing or being overzealous to get positive cancer results to rack up on payments from insurance companies! You gave that girl that man, so just—"

"Just what?" I snapped, pulling the string to my hospital gown. "Let her have my fuckin' husband?"

"Yes!" both of my fake ass sisters yelled in unison.

"We have history!" I frantically slipped into my shoes before grabbing my coat.

"Well, you threw that away, Lottie. You are his past. Let that man be happy with his present!"

"While I'm carrying his future?" I scoffed, sliding into my coat.

"A future you didn't even want with him?" Zailey mockingly scoffed. "Abort that baby and whatever mission you're on, and leave that man and his new woman alone. We're about to take you for these scans for this second opinion that we told your stupid ass to get over a month ago, then we're taking you the fuck home."

* * *

But I didn't go home after my scans. Shit, I didn't even let them take me to my appointment. I took an Uber to my appointment alone so I could call Dr Alex's office and leave a frantic voicemail about how she ruined my fuckin' life. If my sister wasn't going to help me sue that clinic for emotional distress, I'd find another fuckin' lawyer to do that job.

Yes, the news that I was dying turned me cold. Everyone

around me was living their lives normally, and I had to accept that I was about to lose everything. Jacyn's love felt forced, like he was only loving me because he felt like he had to. Like he felt that I needed intensive care, love, and affection because he looked at me as fragile and sickly. Jacyn felt responsible for me. No matter my mood, he always catered to my needs. Maybe if I had loved and appreciated him more, things would've been better. He would've fought to stay. Maybe if I hadn't told him the news the way I did, he would've never gone to the club that night. I pushed him into Melody's arms. She was everything I wasn't, which is probably what drew him to her. Even in her absence, Jacyn didn't try to mend things with me. But with a baby on the way, he was sure to come back. We were family, and Melody could do nothing to compete with that.

 I made a few phone calls that Friday night and ended up at The Whore House with Bonnie. We'd gotten there during the Trap-N-Paint event, so the music wasn't too loud to have a conversation. Bonnie assumed I was there with her to have her back if Kelsius showed up there with some other bitch. Girl, I was there for my own personal reasons, not to be delusional with her. Shit, I had delusions of my own. I didn't tell her that I was pregnant. She'd figure it out when she saw me ordering a Sprite instead of Patrón.

 "If that nigga shows up here with another bitch, I'm blanking on him." Bonnie shook her leg frantically, looking around the club as we sat at the bar. The lunatic even had on pink Tims to go with her pink mini dress. She'd taken her signature hoops from her ears and had her hair up in a bun. She was ready to stomp a shoe print in a bitch.

 I had to laugh a little. "Girl, you stay ready to fight a bitch over Bro. I can see if he was paying all your bills or some shit. In this economy, yeah, I'd fight over a nigga who was paying my bills. But you're rich and got your own. You don't even need him to pay child support, so leave that little boy alone. As long as he takes care of that little baby y'all have together, that's all that matters.

Leave that young nigga the fuck alone. He's barely twenty-one, and you're twenty-six. The principal at Bronzeworth Academy is infatuated with you. He's thirty-two. Go out with him and leave the YN alone."

"Man, Kelsius has a size thirty-two *dick*. You fuck the nigga, then tell me if you can leave him the fuck alone!" Bonnie huffed.

"Shaking my head," I said as I shook my head. "You're not normal, I'm telling you."

"You wouldn't be normal either if a nigga and your rose fucked you on the hood of his Mustang in broad daylight outside of church. That's why I can't go in his mama's church now." Bonnie looked proud of the fact that Ms. Lydia couldn't stand her.

"I don't care how good a nigga fucked me. I'm not fighting over a nigga who made it perfectly clear on several occasions that he wants everyone *but* me," I told her without thinking.

Bonnie looked at me like I wasn't there to fight for a nigga I felt belonged to me as well. "Bitch, aren't you here digging for information on your nigga who ain't your nigga, too? Your sisters have been on your neck about that second opinion, so you can't blame nobody but yourself for that nigga moving on. You were cruel to that man when all he ever did was love you. If Kelsius treated me the way that Jacyn treated you, bitch, I'd bite a bitch for looking at the nigga the wrong way! When you had Joel, Jacyn stayed with you at the hospital the entire time! He slept in the bed with you! He took showers with you and washed your bloody pussy! I couldn't even get Kelsius to cut Bayou's cord! He had the nerve to ask the doctors when my pussy was going to shrink down to normal!"

I couldn't help but chuckle a little. Kelsius was a fool. Little did Bonnie know, Kelsius was somewhere laid up with Izzie that night. Izzie FaceTimed me from the nigga's bed earlier that afternoon while I was getting my scans done. I didn't have the heart to tell Bonnie our friend got the nigga's attention and had been fuckin' him for weeks. I needed Bonnie to come with me to the club. She could fight the nigga's bitches off of him on her own time.

"You're laughing when I'm being fuckin' serious." Bonnie shook her head at me. "Most of us are out here searching for a love that your stupid ass just threw away. Not just threw away, but gave to another bitch! Like, 'here, bitch, have my husband!' I don't give a fuck if you thought you were dying! I would've told the nigga he better jump in that fuckin' casket with me before it closed! Muthafucka, we're going to meet God together!"

I signaled one of the bottle girls to come over. "Excuse me, can I get a Sprite with cherries and grenadine? Thanks."

Bonnie frowned, glancing at the bartender in the skimpy gold bikini before looking back at me. "A Shirley Temple? Bitch, if you don't get a 'Fuck Me in The Ass Sideways'. It's the special for the night. We said we were gonna try that and a 'Big Titty Ho on a Motorcycle'."

I shook my head, glancing at the bottle girl as she made our drinks. Looked like they were short on bartenders that night. The bottle girls were always on the floor, not behind the bar. I looked back at Bonnie. "I'm not in the mood to drink.

Bonnie clicked her teeth. "You should be. You just lost your best hitta. I'd like to see you try to get this nigga back. Have you heard Melody sing? She sounds like a damn siren! She's gonna sing Jacyn's dick right into her pussy, I'm sorry to tell you, baby." Bonnie snickered a little. She was still salty at the fact that I was even considering letting Melody take over the healthcare facilities when I was gone. She'd rather I marry the nigga off to one of my sisters than the bitch who Kelsius once had an infatuation for. Shit, probably still did.

I rolled my eyes as the bartender slid me my drink along with the receipt. "I'll get him back." I sipped from my drink, which tasted so good.

Bonnie squinted at me to get a better view of the slight grin on my face. "The results of your scans came back clear, so I can see why you're happy. You said you wanted to come to the Trap-n-

Paint event, but you don't even smoke hookah, and you can barely even color, so I know you're not here to paint. You've never been a smoker, but I'm not sure why you're not drinking when you should either be celebrating your clear scans or mourning the divorce being finalized. Are you getting surgery this weekend to remove those tumors? Is that why you're not drinking?"

I shook my head, peeping over Bonnie's shoulder as the person I was waiting for made his way over to the bar. "Cousin Donnie!" I squealed, putting my drink down on the counter.

Bonnie frowned, peeping back over her shoulder as Donovan walked up to us at the bar. Bonnie looked my cousin over as Donovan gave me a tight hug before sitting down at the bar on the other side of me. Bonnie gazed at Donovan like Kelsius who?

Donovan was tall, brown, and handsome. Thirty-nine-years-old. Athletic build, like he never missed a day in the gym. Probably the best dressed male on my father's side. He opened a casino a few years back. I'd never seen him with the same woman twice at a family gathering, whenever he came to one. The last time I saw him was last year at Uncle Harvey's funeral. He laid low most of the time. The only reason he came out was that I'd lied to him and said that Melody was there to meet him. He knew the club was run by Dawnna and didn't want to run into her, but he did want to meet his daughter.

"Donnie," I glanced at Bonnie, who was still in a daze, "this is my bestie, Bonnie. Bonnie, this is my cousin, Donnie. *Melody's* father."

The gaze in Bonnie's eyes faded as she looked at me before rolling her light eyes. "Melody's father?" She got up from her stool. "This is why you came here? To meet up with your nigga's new father-in-law?"

I frowned at her. "New what?"

Bonnie grabbed her Prada purse from the bar. "When I left Kelsius's bed this morning, he said that Jacyn plans to marry Melody on fuckin' Monday. She'll be back in town because a fuckin' tree fell on the bitch's grandma's house this morning after that storm we had last night. They're getting fuckin' married, bitch. Stop obsessing over the nigga. He's gone. Deal with it." Bonnie stormed off from the bar.

"Have a good night, bookie-butt," I called out to her.

"Bitch, don't tell me what the fuck to do!" Bonnie yelled back at me.

I didn't know what her problem was. Everything was always all about her. I'd come to the club for my own agenda, not to stalk Kelsius, who probably wasn't coming to the club that night once Izzie put that reverse cowgirl move on the nigga. Niggas would follow that girl home from work after she had a nigga by his ankles, begging her to slow down.

"My daughter's getting married to who now?" Donnie broke my glare from watching Bonnie storm out of the club in those ridiculous pink Tims.

I turned back around on the stool, glancing at my cousin before picking up my drink. "My husband. *Ex*-husband, I guess."

"The shit was on the news this morning," Donnie told me something I didn't know. "You know the Oxberry family stays on the news. I had no idea you were divorcing him, and I definitely have no idea why my daughter—your cousin—is marrying him."

"I set it up," I mumbled under my breath. "I thought I was dying, and I wanted Jacyn to be able to run my mother's healthcare facility. The only way he could inherit it was to marry into the family."

Donnie shook his head before scratching his chin, finger running through his thick beard. "Nah, I'm pretty sure he had to marry into your *mother's* side of the family. Not your father's side. It's Devereaux Industries, not Biggs, baby girl. Who the fuck was the lawyer who helped your mother draft that will? I'm pretty sure he misinterpreted that shit. If something happened to you, and Jacyn had to marry into the family to inherit your share in that company, he would have to marry a Devereaux, I guarantee it."

"So, I matched him with that bitch for no reason anyway?" I

had to laugh out loud at how careless I had been throughout the entire process. And how incompetent my circle of professionals was. First, my doctor mixes up my files. Then, the will—which I didn't even read, if I'm being honest, because I trusted what my father and lawyers interpreted.

"That bitch is my daughter," Donnie growled. "And you said she'd be here."

"No one's seen her in over a month. She used to teach at Joel's school. She was a music teacher. She used to work here, too. She ran this bar. Used to sing to the guests. Had all these niggas mesmerized. This is where I met her." I sighed, realizing that I was sitting in the same spot that I was sitting in when I met Melody that Friday night back in August.

"Can't believe Latisha had her granddaughter working here. Latisha used to pimp out her daughter." Donnie frowned, his thick eyebrows intertwining. "Dawnna shouldn't even have let Melody work here. Stupid bitches. Let me find out she was pimping out my fuckin' daughter. A daughter I didn't even know I had until you told me last month."

I hated to tell the nigga, but I had to also tell him about Jaliyah. "She had another daughter, ya know."

Donnie looked at me. "Another daughter? How old is *she*?"

"Fifteen. Which means Dawnna had to have had Jaliyah when she was around—"

"Eighteen. When she left Texas. She told me she lost my baby." Donnie looked at me as I shrugged, drinking from my glass.

"She did. She gave Jaliyah up to the system. Jaliyah was a patient at one of my facilities. She's no longer there, though," I mentioned before he could ask to see her. "DSS removed her from our custody after she tried to give herself a C-section to remove a baby that her foster father put in her."

Donnie looked at me with a blank stare before his jaws tightened and twitched. "Where the fuck is this foster father?"

"In jail," I assured him. "The foster mother, too, who apparently watched her husband have sex with her. They wanted another baby. The plan was to get Jaliyah pregnant and take custody of the baby once it was born. There's an ongoing investigation to see whether they were trafficking babies from their home. There's evidence that two of their other foster kids may have delivered as well and—"

Donnie held his hand up to me to stop talking. He looked over at the other end of the bar, signaling one of the young bartenders to come over. "I need a fuckin' drink," he muttered.

"You don't want to paint? I got us a booth." I tried not to smirk.

"Paint?" Donnie looked at me like I'd lost what little of my mind I had left. "Don't fuckin' play with me." He looked back at the young bartender as she approached him. "Where is the owner?"

The bartender paused, looking at Donnie like she'd seen a ghost. "You-You own The Clover!" Her eyes grew wide. "That casino in Concord!"

Donnie wasn't in the mood for any groupie love that night. "Can you get the owner? Tell her Donovan wants her to make him a drink."

The bartender nodded frantically before rushing off.

Donnie sat there cracking his knuckles.

"You got Dawnna pregnant when she was twelve years old, Donnie," I reminded him. "You were eighteen. The fuck were you doing fuckin' on a twelve-year-old girl?"

Donnie looked at me like I had no idea who the fuck I was questioning. "Lil cuz, you need to mind your fuckin' business. You're already mixing up some shit by telling me to meet you in a place I didn't want to come to."

"The Biggs family is known to prey on young women. They made you a predator, too, huh?" I scoffed.

"You have no idea what Dawnna went through back then. It was either my father or me. Or my uncles. *Your* father included." Donnie watched me shake my head. "A lot of poking went on at their poker games, and Latisha provided the entertainment. Dawnna's father practically sold her to our family. I left Louisiana and went to Texas to live with my cousin. I didn't even know Dawnna left New Orleans after the storm. I didn't see her until five years later. Had no idea she'd been in Houston. I had a fiancée and a five-year-old daughter when I ran back into Dawnna."

My heart jumped in my chest. "You have *another* daughter, nigga?"

"I took Dawnna out to eat that night, one thing led to another, and we slept together. Then, she disappeared on me," Donnie went on to explain. "Didn't leave a number or anything. The shit fucked me up. I ended up breaking up with my fiancée after all the plans we made. I didn't see Dawnna again until I ran into her while she was serving tables at an Olive Garden. She looked like she was ready to pop. Said she was eight months pregnant. I made her give me her number, so she'd call me when she was in labor. And she did. She told me she had a fuckin' stillborn. That she held the dead baby in her arms. That she'd named that baby Jaliyah. That she was our second baby that she'd lost."

I watched Donnie get up from the stool. "I thought you were having a drink?"

Donnie chuckled, straightening out the collar on his blazer. "You've always been a messy little bitch. The next time I see you, my daughters better be with you. Don't waste my fuckin' time again." He walked away from the bar.

"Bye, cuzzo." I looked back over my shoulder, watching as he walked toward the dance floor

"Fuck you," Donnie snarled back, strolling his way through the crowd.

CHAPTER 2
Lottie

I turned back around to face the bar, watching that giddy bartender come from the doorway behind the bar. Dawnna stopped in the doorway, spotting me sitting at the bar. The light in the bartender's eyes faded when she approached me, noticing that Donnie was no longer sitting beside me.

"Damn, where's Donnie?" She pursed her thick lips at me before looking back at Dawnna, who huffed, making her way over to us as she tied an apron around her waist.

"This bitch," Dawnna said loud enough for me to hear as she strutted over to the bartender's side, facing me.

Dawnna was a fine-ass bitch, I have to admit. There aren't many women in the city of Charlotte fuckin' with this bitch on her worst day. Tall, chocolate brown, dimples, long natural hair, seductive eyes, naturally long eyelashes, flawless fuckin' skin. If she ever got a hold of your man, I promise you he's never coming back home.

"Hey, Dawnna." I faked a smile, sliding my empty glass to the tiny bartender so she could fix me another drink. I looked into Dawnna's angry expression. "You just missed my cousin, Donnie. You know, your baby daddy? The nigga who didn't even *know* he was your baby daddy. I might've slipped up and told him about

Melody marrying my nigga and Jaliyah being locked away at another mental institution. Come to find out, ya baby daddy has *another* daughter. Daddy's girls. What do you think about throwing them a little reunion right here at this club? We can turn this place into a gala or something. Have your little prostitutes stop selling pussy for one night to serve food."

The bartender snatched my glass, eyes widening as she looked at Dawnna for a reaction before looking back at me like I had no idea who I was talking to. Dawnna didn't scare me. I was related to the Biggs family. The same family I'd heard Dawnna had been passed around to while the majority of my family lived in Louisiana.

"Keep talking shit, and I'ma sell your pussy too. Dreeka, how much you think I'll get for a cancer survivor?" Dawnna nudged the bartender as she made me another Shirley Temple.

Dreeka looked me over and shrugged. "Depends. You think all that radiation and chemo dried up her pussy? It's probably fried like bacon."

Dawnna agreed. "Probably. That's why her husband wasn't too fucked up about divorcing it."

The smile on my face quickly faded. Oh, she had to go there. "I wonder what my uncles are doing tonight. Which one was it who turned you out? Or should I say which two or three? Or did my cousin save you by doing to you what they all wanted to do? My cousin had you out here popping out babies like puppies. Your daughter is basically a year and a half younger than you in dog years, just like a pit bull bitch in heat. My entire male bloodline talks about you when they get drunk, ya know. They all remember the twelve-year-old bitch who'd suck their dick and take the money they paid her back to your daddy. How is your daddy anyway, sweetheart? Where is he?"

"Your cousin Donavon sent him to A Street Cemetery, little white girl," Dawnna let me know, as she pulled out the rolled blunt she had tucked between her plump breasts. "Keep fuckin with me *or* that man, and you'll end up there, too. How a bitch who was supposed to be dead weeks ago standing here, trying to get muthafuckas to join in her misery? You should've put all this energy into keeping that sexy nigga to yourself instead of handing him to my daughter. I guess you must've gotten some good news from your doctor, and you think that starting shit with my family will get *your* family back together." She scoffed, looking me over as she put her blunt to her lips. "That nigga is gone, white baby doll. You heard what they say. Once you go black..."

Dreeka smirked, sliding my drink over to me before she left the area to serve another customer.

I glared at her before glaring back at Dawnna. "I'm pregnant," I told the bitch.

Dawnna laughed between her teeth as she put a lighter to her blunt. A high flame sparked the blunt, sizzling as she pulled from it. She inhaled before exhaling sharply, smoke surrounding her, floating my way. "So, what you think? That baby is gonna make him come back? You really think having a baby will keep a nigga who doesn't wanna be kept? A baby won't bring him back."

"I guess you would know all about that. That's why you just tossed your kids to the system. Having this baby might not make Jacyn come home, but it'll make your daughter leave him the fuck alone," I hissed, waving the smoke away from my face. "I will be the cancer-surviving babymama from hell."

Dawnna pulled from the blunt again before taking it from her lips. Smoke left her nose as she shook her head in disgust. "You had a good man, Savannah. A *good* man. Hurt men don't come back. His final act of love was leaving you where you had him fucked up."

"Watch me get him back," I assured her, and she laughed out loud.

"My daughter thinks she can make moves and her mother not know exactly where she is. Jacyn has plans for my oldest baby. He doesn't plan on leaving her alone. He's been making plans to keep her in his life. Plans nobody can stop, but God, *maybe*. I can point you to her, tell you where she's gonna be Monday if you actually think you can compete with her."

I tried not to look too eager, but I guess my facial expression showed I was desperate to stop whatever plans Jacyn had for that bitch.

Dawnna set her blunt down in a crystal ashtray on the cherry wood bar. She nodded over my shoulder, and I looked behind me in the direction she was nodding. "You see those security guards over there? My mama hired them to follow my daughter around like a puppy. And when they can't follow her, they send their sons to follow her. And when their sons can't follow her, they send their friends. One of their sons' friends is your ex-brother-in-law, Jacob."

I looked back at her, frowning. "Jacyn's adopted brother?"

Dawnna rolled her pretty eyes. "Oh, so you *do* have a brain after all that chemo? You wanna know where my daughter is, just follow Jacob. He should be here in a few, after the Paint-N-Sip. Sit down, grab a brush, maybe paint yourself a picture of a new man. Jacyn isn't coming back, boo. Welcome to single motherhood." She chuckled as she walked away from me, headed over to the opposite end of the bar where her bartenders stood, preparing for a busy night ahead of them.

As soon as Dawnna walked away, I pulled out my phone and flipped through my contacts until I saw Jacob's name. I started texting.

I mouthed to myself as I texted him, "Nigga, don't play with me."

A few seconds after I hit send, I saw those three dots moving. After a few seconds, the movement stopped. Whatever smart shit he wanted to say, he changed his mind.

I sat at the bar that night, waiting for Jacob to show up. And just like the bitch said, he came strolling into the club, right on over to the bar. Sexy, brown skinned, clean-cut nigga. He looked and smelled rich. He was the audio engineer of the musical family. The one who produced most of their music. He'd co-written a few songs with Jacyn. And like Jacyn, Jacob had ghostwritten for a few R&B artists. He'd written love songs that had won Grammys. A few of the songs he'd written were about our brief encounters in the past. Encounters no one knew about but me, him, and God.

Jacob slid onto a barstool, three seats away from me. He didn't look my way but started having a conversation with the pretty bartender.

Dreeka's eyes lit up when she saw him. She flicked the blonde curls of her wig over her shoulder as she approached him, her forearms resting on the bar. "You coming to my birthday party on Monday night?" she asked him.

Jacob looked Dreeka's pretty face over as she leaned in a little closer to pretend she couldn't hear him unless she was inches from his face. "Depends on how late big bro has me out. I'm gonna be a witness at the courthouse."

I stirred my drink, shaking my leg anxiously.

"Courthouse?" she spoke over the music. "What he do? The nigga caught a charge?"

Jacob chuckled. "Nah, he's getting married again to that chocolate thang who used to work here."

Dreeka sort of glanced at me before giggling, standing up from leaning on the bar. "Oh, you're talking about Jacyn?" Her eyes grew bigger as if she was trying to hint to Jacob that the nigga's ex-wife was sitting a few feet from him.

Jacob ignored her cues. "Yeah. Shawty been gone for over a month and a half. I found out she was selling her grandmother's house. A tree fell on the muthafucka, so she's gotta come back to town to have it fixed before she can put the house up for sale. Jacyn's going to get his woman back, convinced he's getting married at about 3:00 on Monday. That stripper, BeeBee, helped bro pick out the wedding dress and everything. Me and her are supposed to be witnesses to this crazy union. She told me she paid for a suite at the Ritz and shit. Put the room in bro's name. He said they were headed over there around 5:00.

Mama said some shit about having a gala for them around 8:00. If I don't stay out too late that night, I'll come through. Sure, they'll be late to the party, ya know, with baby girl being a virgin and all."

Dreeka clapped and cheered like she was the one about to get my husband's dick. "My boss lady's daughter is finally getting broken in, huh?"

"Yeah, she's getting fucked that night." Jacob exhaled sharply, watching Dreeka twerk a little to the idea of my man fuckin' her boss's daughter.

"Aye!" Dreeka clapped her cheeks together. "I know he's taking her somewhere romantic for their honeymoon. I've been to your mama's church. Your brother can fuckin' *sing*. I bet he'll sing that girl into an orgasm, whew!"

The bitch just kept rubbing it in.

Even Jacob started to look irritated by the fact that she was talking about his brother fuckin' another woman when his ex-wife was sitting right there. "They're on their newlywed shit, so I'm sure I won't be at mama's dinner too long." He looked at his watch. "But I'll holla at ya, Dreeka. Gotta meet my crew outside to make sure the guards at the front know they're in VIP with me tonight. Lil fine shit." He bit his lip, his gaze planted on her lips. "You look good tonight."

Dreeka flicked her hair over her shoulder, smacking her lips. "So come over then, nigga. Don't act like you don't know where the fuck I stay."

"Will I need to bring my gun?" Jacob questioned, though the way he was gazing at her like he wanted to pull on her wig while he bent her over, I doubted her response mattered.

"Probably," she admitted. "You ask that question like you would ever go anywhere without it."

Jacob was satisfied with the answer. "Text me when you get off. I'll pull up." He rubbed her arm a little before getting up from the stool, watching her ass bounce in those shorts as she walked toward the opposite end of the counter.

Jacob turned toward me and winked as he walked past me and away from the bar.

I waited about a minute or two before I got up from the bar. My anxiety was on full throttle mode as I left the club. I actually thought stirring up Donnie and Dawnna's past would make me feel better, but all I did was stir up shit from my own past. The plan was to get Donnie to take me on a search for his daughter. I didn't know Dawnna's minions were connected to Jacob. I barely spoke to Jacob. Though our past encounters were brief, the ripple effect of the moment still affected me four years later.

"Stop calling her phone. She's getting fucked tonight," Jacob's voice sang over my shoulder as soon as I stepped outside the club's doors.

I rolled my eyes, turning around to see Jacob standing alongside the brick building, shaking hands with one of the security guards before he walked toward me. I huffed, turning back around to make my way to my car.

"Boy, shut the fuck up," I muttered, strutting down the sidewalk, annoyed by the intoxicating signature scent of Jacob's cologne. The entire male bloodline of the Oxberry family wore that spicy, warm fragrance. One of their uncles owned a perfumery and gifted out the cologne to the men of the family every time a new fragrance dropped. The scent was definitely a panty dropper.

"This is what you wanted, right? For bro to move on?" Jacob caught up with me.

"I wanted my mama's company run by someone who's competent," I snapped. "Where is he?"

"Packing his spinnanight bag." Jacob chuckled. "Your lil cousin is selling her mama's house. She thinks she's moving away, but Jacyn's not gonna let that happen. You should see the dress he picked out for her. I'll take some pictures, send 'em to ya phone. Ya know, so you can put them in your family album."

"Jacob, I will cut you out here." I glanced at the stupid smirk on his face.

"I'll text you when they get to the hotel, baby girl." Jacob grabbed my arm, pulling my body toward his.

I snatched away before looking around to see if anyone was watching him touching me. I looked back up at him. All six feet of pure chocolate. "Where is my son right now?" I asked him.

"With Moms." He frowned a little, temples twitching. "He's getting big. I bought him some new clothes. A few sensory toys. I'll have Joel while ya ex is on his honeymoon."

"Don't have any of your bitches around my son," I warned him, pointing in his face.

"*Our* son will be around whoever I'm around," he snarled at me. "Just worry about my text. And I'll worry about the rest."

I folded my arms, the cold October breeze blowing through my hair.

"Heard you had a second opinion today. You know word travels. Guessing you got some good news. Good news for Joel." Jacob scoffed.

"Bad news for Melody," I assured him.

"Leave that girl alone. Dawnna made some mistakes, but one mistake she won't make is letting you fuck with her daughter. Either of her daughters. So, chill out, aight?" Jacob leaned in and whispered.

"Nigga, just send that text." I huffed before turning around to walk away from him.

* * *

"You need to leave these people the fuck alone." Izzie huffed, pulling up in front of the Ritz-Carlton the following Monday evening.

Jacob had sent the text about thirty minutes ago that Jacyn had tied the fuckin' knot with Melody. I couldn't wait to tie that fuckin' knot around Melody's neck.

I tightened the belt on my trench coat, eyeing people going in and coming out of the hotel lobby doors. "Like you need to leave

Bonnie's nigga alone, huh?" I rolled my eyes. Izzie was the last bitch to judge me when I'd just witnessed her walking out the back door of Kelsius's house on their family compound.

Izzie laughed resentfully. "Bitch, what? Kelsius is not that hoe's nigga, just like Jacyn is not yours. You might as well take that wedding ring off, melt it down into some earrings or something. You wanted that man to move on, and now that he has, you want him back? That nigga wanted you when you were sick. Waited on you hand and foot like you were his fuckin' queen! And you tossed him away! You know I fucked your family lawyer, right? The nigga pillowtalks. He said Jacyn practically begged you not to leave him in front of your family, and you just shoved papers in his face for him to sign!"

I didn't want to hear any more. I grabbed my folder with the documents to prove that I'd made a mistake in letting him go and reached for the door handle. "Just keep the car running. I won't be long."

"You can't be this fuckin' controlling!" Izzie yelled as I got out of the car, slamming the door behind me.

Though I played it cool, I was a nervous wreck. I didn't even know what I was doing there. Jacyn barely knew that bitch. The bitch I handed him to, not knowing he'd already met her. He had his mind set on getting to know Melody before I'd even introduced them. He'd met her the day I told him my diagnosis. She was probably the entire reason he didn't crash out that night.

Forty-five days had gone by since the day they'd met. She'd barely known Jacyn for five days when he signed the divorce papers. Forty days had gone by with no contact with the nigga, and they were married. Jacob's petty ass sent me pictures of Jacyn kissing that bitch in front of the magistrate. It was one of those deep Hollywood kisses. Ya know, where the man grabs her close and bends forward, leaning the woman all the way back in a poetic embrace. I could tell the picture was genuine. He couldn't wait to kiss that bitch. He'd bought that pretty pink dress to match that pink wedding band on her finger. He put thought into their big day. He used to put thought into loving me, and I didn't appreciate it until I saw him doing the shit to someone else.

"Hi," I faked a smile as I approached the front desk associate. "My husband, Jacyn Oxberry, says he left a key for me at the front desk. He said he booked an executive suite." I watched the associate search the computer for his name.

When she found his name, she nodded. "Oh, yes, Mr. Oxberry checked in a few minutes ago, but he didn't leave any keys." She looked from the computer monitor into my face. "He looked like he just came from a wedding ceremony. Maybe I should call his room and let him know you're here. What was your name again?"

I laughed off my irritation with the nosy bitch. "Maybe I should call my cousin, Brawnson Biggs, who works at the corporate office, and let him know that his minimum-wage-making front desk associate is worrying about business that doesn't concern her. What was *your* name again? Patty Pankcakes?" I eyed the bitch's nametag before looking back into her chubby face.

Patty Pancakes pursed her lips. "My name is Patty Paxton," she corrected me.

"Whatever," I snapped. "Can I have the key to my husband's suite, or do I have to get you fired? So you can't pay the rent at that based-on-your-income apartment that I know you stay in with your nigga who's not even on your lease. Who's making you work to pay all the bills while he's home, wearing out your couch from Goodwill. Probably fuckin' one of your hood rat friends through that dusty couch." I watched the sensitive bitch scramble to activate a room key for me. "Worry about your nigga, not mine."

"He's not yours, obviously," the bitch muttered.

"What was that?" I pretended not to hear her while I made a mental note of the fatty's name. Was dead serious about reporting her ass to the corporate office.

"Here are your room keys." She faked a smile, slapping the

keys onto the counter. "The room number is 1532 on the 15th floor. Enjoy your night."

I rolled my eyes and grabbed the keys before prancing across the marble floor toward the elevators. With each floor the elevator passed, I grew more nervous. I really had no idea what the fuck I was going to say, but I knew I had to say something. The moment the elevator door opened, I spotted Jacyn on the other end of the hallway, ice bucket in his hand. I waited until he turned the corner before I made my way to his room. I took a few deep breaths before I tapped on the door. After a few seconds, the door opened. And there Melody and I were, staring into each other's faces.

"You gonna just make me stand in the doorway, or are you gonna let me the fuck in?" I disguised my nervousness with animosity.

Melody tightened her towel, looking at me like I'd lost my mind coming to ruin her little honeymoon. "What do you want?"

I shoved the folder at her.

"What is this?" She asked, flipping through the pages in the folder.

I briefly explained to the bitch that my records had been mixed up with another patient's records and that I was cancer-free. That I didn't have inflammatory breast cancer. I watched her open the folder to flip through the scans and the doctor's summary. Once I saw that she'd gotten to the page that showed my bloodwork results, I smiled and said, "Oh, and according to my bloodwork, I'm pregnant."

Melody's hands shook as she sighed slowly, sharply closing the folder. She probably wanted to throw the shit at my face. "We haven't even been married an hour, Scarlett. It's not too late to get an annulment. You want your nigga back this bad? To follow us to a hotel room moments after he told the court and God that death couldn't even keep him from me?"

The smile on my face faded.

"I do believe his vows to me went something like: 'Melody

Blues Morgan, I promise from this day forward to learn, to love, to hold, to breathe, to honor, and to cherish you. To make this last. Whatever needs to be done, I promise to do it. I will be your peace, your provider, your protector, and your partner. I'll laugh with you on your best days and comfort you on your worst days. I can't wait to dream with you, celebrate with you, and create life with you. You are every prayer that I prayed, every laugh that I laughed, every song that I sang, every promise that I made. On this day, I give you all of me in exchange for all of you. I pray for anyone who comes between us. No weapon formed against us will prosper. With these rings, we are one. Can I kiss my bride?'" She smiled at the memory of what happened an hour before she was standing in front of me, telling me that bullshit.

"I thought I was fuckin' dying, Melody." I interrupted her mushy thoughts with why I'd paid her a visit in that expensive suite. "My battle isn't over. I'm still here. I still have a fuckin' chance. I want him back."

Melody gripped the folder in her hands. "You have some fuckin' balls coming here. The last thing I need is a charge right now, but I know plenty of bitches who don't mind going to jail for stomping that baby right out of you."

"Aye," Jacyn's voice echoed through the hallway. "The fuck are you doing here, Lottie?"

Melody's eyes watered as she shoved the folder into my chest before she walked away from the door and back into the room.

I glared at her before looking at Jacyn as he approached me. When I thought he was going to cuss me the fuck out for coming to his hotel room, he walked past me and into the room to check on Melody. He wanted to know her mental state. Make sure that whatever happened while he was away wasn't affecting her. Fuck me at the moment; it was about protecting her, and that hurt.

"Melody, what did she say to you?" Jacyn tried to grab a hold of her, but she shoved him away.

"Ask her!" Melody shouted, going over to a shopping bag that was on the coffee table in the center of the room. "Ask her why she's here! Ask her what's in that fuckin' folder!"

"Baby, I'm asking *you*." Jacyn's voice was calm as always. "You gotta calm down and talk to me. Breathe, and talk to me."

Melody's breathing shook as she did as he instructed and tried to calm down. "She went out of her way to come here as soon as we left the courthouse. Ask *that* bitch why she's here. I'm done, Jacyn."

Jacyn shook his head. "We just started."

"Well, *she* just ended it!" Melody snapped, digging through the *Pink* shopping bag. She grabbed the first thing she could find, which was a pair of lounge pants. She jumped into the pants, letting her towel fall to the floor. I knew the bitch was bad, but seeing her standing there in pants and no shirt, I could see why Jacyn wasn't trying to let the slut go. She looked like she was built in a black Barbie factory. Whew, I was so happy I stopped that nigga from cracking that bitch's eggs that evening.

"Don't go, Melody." Jacyn found himself begging another woman not to leave him when he needed her most.

"This was a mistake." She slipped into an off-the-shoulder sweatshirt before slipping into some cute pink Crocs that she removed from the bag. Then, she turned to Jacyn, snatching her wedding rings from her finger and shoving them into his chest.

Jacyn grabbed her wrist, pulling her body to his. "Mellie, talk to me. Don't do this."

Melody shoved Jacyn off her before grabbing her phone from the coffee table. "Go back to your wife. Help that bitch with your kids. You didn't want the divorce in the first place, remember?"

Jacyn's eyes followed Melody as she walked past me and out the door. He didn't even look my way. He slid Melody's wedding rings into his pants pocket before heading back toward the bedroom. I stepped inside the hotel room, closing the door behind me. I knew Jacyn all too well. He rarely ever overreacted. He always thought before making any moves. He always gave a person a chance to cool down and rethink their decisions.

I knew he didn't plan to let Melody go that easily after the wedding vows Melody just said the nigga made to her. The only thing that muthafucka said to me at our wedding ceremony was, "I do." No written vows. Barely a grin on his face. My period was on that day, and my hair kept frizzing up. My make-up artist forgot my fuckin' setting spray, so I had a make-up stain on my dress. The caterers were late. My mama and aunt got into a fight over whose greens tasted the fuckin' best. My wedding day was a disaster. I was a mess, and Jacyn tried to comfort me, but I wouldn't let him. And there I was, ruining his wedding day again.

Jacyn came back into the living area, sliding into his crisp dress shirt. "What the fuck is in that folder, Scarlett?" he asked as he went over and sat on the couch.

I approached him with the folder and handed it to him. "My second opinion."

Jacob laughed without cracking a smile. "The test you should've gotten before you told me to move on and remarry? Oh, okay."

"I don't have breast cancer," I said, watching him flip the folder open. "I scheduled the date to have my spinal tumors removed. I also scheduled my first prenatal appointment." I watched him take a deep breath before he looked up at me.

"You weren't on birth control?" Jacyn asked me, his eyebrows furrowing.

"We barely had sex. I wasn't thinking about pregnancy. I was thinking about one last time with my husband before I told him it was over!" I exclaimed.

"You didn't want any more kids," Jacyn reminded me. "I specifically remember you telling me that if you ever found out that you were pregnant, you'd get rid of the baby before you even let me find out. What's changed?"

It was official. Jacyn agreeing with an abortion was the equivalent of when pigs fly. Jacyn dreamed of having a big family, and my health always fucked that up for him. Under different circumstances, the news that I was pregnant would've been music to his ears. But those days, the only music on his mind had lyrics that didn't include my name. The new lyrics to his song just walked the fuck out of the hotel room.

"I made a mistake," I whispered, watching him forcefully drop the folder onto the coffee table. "I still love you, Jacyn. I know you love me, too. You can't possibly love a bitch you barely know, Jacyn. You're lying if you tell me you love a bitch who you haven't even spent a week with!"

Jacyn leaned back in the chair. "You never knew how love worked. You never knew how to love me. That woman who just walked out that door knows how to love. We touched before we even touched. That's how I know I can love her. That's how I know I need her. That's how I know she's mine. *All* fuckin' mine."

My heart instantly pounded in my chest. "I don't give a fuck about that marriage certificate or those pretty pink rings you gave that bitch. You belong to me, Jacyn! I've known you all my life! You wouldn't have even known the bitch had I not told you it was over! You would've never left me! You would've stayed with me forever, and you fuckin' know it! I'm all you know! Less than a week of foreplay doesn't make her a fuckin wife!"

Jacyn sat there calmly, collecting his thoughts. He knew I loved to pick arguments when I felt I wasn't getting the attention I felt I deserved. That made him fight even harder to not give me the satisfaction of pissing him off. "That first night that Melody and I spent together, we slept together but didn't have sex. It was the best sleep I'd had in a long time. The only time I woke up was to make sure she was still there, lying next to me. Everything about her and with her feels like home. The home I never had, living in that big ass mansion with you."

"Nigga, you can't be this stupid!" I huffed. "You don't even know this bitch! You're moving too fuckin' fast!"

"But isn't that what the fuck you wanted me to do?" Jacyn questioned me. "Wasn't it you who said you wanted a divorce? Who lied to the court about us being separated for a year so we could wrap that shit up? You wasn't moving slow when you shoved those divorce papers at me. So why the fuck do I gotta move slow with her? If me and her were both feeling each other's vibes from the jump, there was no point in taking it slow. My attention span is about as short as your sister Zailey's hair when she takes that wig off. We got to know each other, we liked each other, she's mine, I'm hers, it feels good, let's get married."

I didn't care if I was the one who initiated the shit; I didn't like how enthralled he was with that bitch. Feels good, my fuckin' ass. "Everything feels good when you first meet a person! This chapter is called the fuckin' honeymoon phase!" I exclaimed, feeling like breaking everything in that $1000-per-night room.

"Nah, this chapter is called the beginning." Jacyn corrected me. "The foundation. My family isn't going to control this relationship the way that our family controlled ours. Melody is a decision that I made on my own. I married her for myself, not for Devereaux Industries. I'm glad these results say you're here to stay. Our son needs his mother."

It took everything in me not to tell the nigga that Joel wasn't his. That one drunken night after I'd finished a round of chemo led to me fuckin' his adoptive brother in the back seat of his car. Jacyn and I hadn't touched in months. He was away at a family business meeting. Two weeks later, I went in for my physical and found out I was pregnant. I'd surprised Jacyn that night when he got home with a candlelight dinner. I fucked him like I was trying to fuck Jacob's baby out of me. Three weeks later, I told Jacyn we were pregnant. I'd never seen Jacyn look so happy. I didn't tell Jacob about our son until the day our son was diagnosed with autism when he was two years old. Jacob pretended he didn't even hear me, but he put in an effort to be a major part of Joel's life. He pretended like we never happened. And so did I.

"Even though you're fuckin' up the vibes, I'm glad you're here, though." Jacyn sat up on the couch before leaning forward to rest his forearms on his thighs. He looked up at me as he intertwined his fingers together. "I'm starting my own clinic for music therapy. I put in my two-week notice at your family's company."

"Put in your two weeks' fuckin notice at *my* family's company?" I couldn't believe the nigga.

Jacyn looked up at me, studying my expression as usual. "This is business, right? That's all we've ever been. Loving you never felt like anything more than business. This, what I have with Melody, feels like pleasure."

"I didn't want it to be like this," I admitted. "I just wanted to be at peace with dying, and I didn't want you feeling sorry for me!"

Jacyn frowned at me. "You were my wife. I was trying to comfort you. I didn't want to let go, but I'm glad I did. You say you wanted fuckin' peace? You don't think *I* needed peace? You don't think *I* needed comfort while I was trying to comfort your ungrateful ass? You didn't think that *I* needed a safe space? Even if you didn't push this divorce to be finalized so quickly, we wouldn't have worked out, and do you know why we wouldn't have worked out? Because we both put you first. You're not mad that I'm moving on. You're mad because I survived. You're mad because I became someone else. I'm not the same Jacyn I was before you broke things off that night. You fucked me at that park, then you said fuck me. And even though it hurt my fuckin' soul at the time, I needed that shit. I needed *this* shit. I needed Melody. This," Jacyn tapped the folder on the table, "won't keep me from her. I'm not letting her go. I let you go, but I promise, even death isn't keeping me from her. As soon as you walk out that door, I'm going after her."

The nigga was too sprung on a bitch he hadn't had sex with. He had to have had a piece of her chocolate. There was no way he felt that connected to a woman his body hadn't connected to. It was sex that drew him to her. It had to be that simple. There was no other explanation. As far as I knew, I was the only woman Jacyn had ever had sex with. As honest and truthful as he was raised to be, I doubt he ever cheated on me. He would have come clean. He wasn't a liar.

So, I had to ask him. "Did you fuck her? Is that why you're acting so dumb right now? Niggas claim that bitches go crazy over dick, but y'all act just as stupid over the right pussy. Did you fuck her?"

Jacyn looked me in the eyes and said, "If I fucked her the way I wanted to, she wouldn't have had the energy to walk out the door the way she just did. The plan was to come here, get our first round in, then take her to properly meet my family. She was scared. I couldn't get her to relax. So, I had to go get some ice to cool her off. We were in the middle of a session, and I could feel her nerves. Her body trembled under mine. I want her to enjoy me, not fear me. I slid inside, and she tensed up. She felt like … you know, when the mac-n-cheese touches the yams on a Thanksgiving plate? That's how she feels. And you interrupted. I was supposed to come back to the room and have her open that box that's on that desk over there. Since you're here, I'll let you open it."

If I wanted to play games, Jacyn was going to turn that shit on expert mode. I didn't know why I was dumb enough to walk my ass over there to that desk and open that white box that was topped with a pretty pink ribbon. I pulled the ribbon from the box before removing the lid. I felt my throat damn near close after I let out a loud gasp. Inside the box was a pink diamond slip chain. If you are unaware of what a slip chain necklace is, it's a style of jewelry with a length that can be adjusted using a sliding clasp or an O-ring. In this case, the necklace had a heart-ring. The necklace can be worn as a longer pendant or a choker. One end of the chain is threaded through the heart-ring and slid to its desired length. The necklace is mainly used as what's known as a "day collar" for submissives.

Jacyn never introduced me to that lifestyle, but just about every woman in the Oxberry family wore that style of necklace under their clothing to symbolize their commitment to their dominant partner. That necklace wasn't coming off unless that man took that shit off. Jacyn was pissing me off more by the minute.

Just when I spun around, about to throw that shit at his fuckin' face, I eyed him sitting up straight on the couch, gun in his lap. There he was. The Jacyn who was hidden behind medicine and that doctorate degree. Twenty-five years old with a degree that took most twelve years after high school to achieve. He'd graduated high school with credits toward an associate degree. He was a psychiatrist who prescribed music instead of medicine. He hated how medicine had a hold on him. Without medication, that calm demeanor was nonexistent.

Jacyn suffered from dissociative identity disorder. According to Miss Lydia, doctors say the disorder is in response to seeing his mother die while giving birth, and her body just being tossed into the water, umbilical cord still hanging out of her. While Jacyn was helping me fight through my storms, he was weathering his own storms. He let so much shit go to keep the peace, but all that did was start a war inside him. And the battle was starting there in that room with me.

"You throw that shit, there will be no you, there will be no baby, there will be no one coming between me and my peace," Jacyn warned me, gripping the gun.

"Yeah, except the criminal justice system." I barely got the words out before he cocked the barrel. "Did-did you take your meds today?"

"Why? You scared?" Jacyn snarled.

"Use your coping skills, Jacyn." I gave him the same advice that Jacyn gave the consumers at our facilities.

"My coping skill just walked the fuck out that door." Jacyn got up from the couch.

I gulped, fearful yet turned on a little. The Jacyn he was becoming was definitely a Jacyn I hadn't met. Five days with that bitch, and Jacyn was a brand new man. A man who forgot to pop those 300 milligrams of Seroquel and 15 milligrams of Abilify.

"You don't need her," I whispered.

"Nah, I don't need *you*." Jacyn walked toward me. "Put my baby's necklace down before I choke you with that shit."

I didn't dare turn my back on him. I reached behind me, dropping the box on the table. "It's not over, Jacyn." The tears I didn't want to cry escaped, sliding down my cheeks.

"That's not what you said last month. You promised me forever, and the moment you felt out of control, you said fuck me. Now, I'm saying fuck you. I talked to God in tears the day you told me it was over. There's no coming back from that. If you come near my wife, there will be no words, just bullets. Now get the fuck out." Jacyn mushed my head with the barrel of the gun. "I won't ask again."

CHAPTER 3
Melody

"Bitch!" Belle shoved the shit out of my arm that night in the dressing room at The Midnight Ballet. "Do you have any idea what I had to go through to get that money for that fuckin' hotel room? You got me feeling like Stoney when she let Nate fuck her for Stevie's tuition money when the nigga didn't even get in!"

Belle was so mad that she was putting on entirely too much shimmering body oil. "Belle, if you put on any more oil, you're gonna slide off that pole. You remember when Big Shirley slid off that pole and into the crowd? Almost put Mr. Berry's eye out with her Manolos. And you only have one nipple ring in."

Belle looked down at her double Ds before rolling her big eyes up at me. "The nigga I fucked the other night to pay for your hotel swallowed the muthafucka. I sucked his spine through his dick for that fuckin' room. Do you have any idea how hard it is to do that grip thing on a nigga who barely has enough dick to fuck me? You better get back to that room and toot it up for Jacyn. Or I will! Shit, one of us is getting fucked tonight in that room!"

"I told you the bitch showed up with clear scans and positive pregnancy results! Would you be in the mood to fuck a nigga after his ex-wife shows up, talking about she's pregnant with the nigga's baby? You expect me to still be horny after that shit?" I exclaimed, watching Belle stretch the strings to her bra top behind her back. She was dressed in what she called her lucky green fit. She was working a Monday night, something she never did, to get her money back.

"Man, fuck that bitch and that baby!" The tallest stripper, Blossom, walked by, ass jiggling like Jello.

Belle nodded frantically in agreement. "Hell yeah, fuck boffofem! You married a nigga that you didn't even spend a week with to inherit a company that neither of you is getting because the bitch isn't dead! You couldn't possibly think this shit was going to go smoothly. You don't even know anything about the nigga. What's his favorite color? What's his middle name? Did he eat glue in kindergarten? Was he at the popular table, or did he sit with the nerds in high school? Does the nigga eat pussy from the back?"

I watched as Belle got herself together before she was called out on stage. "That bitch found out where we were having our honeymoon! I was already embarrassed about not being able to..."

Belle stopped tying her bikini bottom. "Not being able to what? Take dick? Girl, you better ride that dick with your throat!"

"That dick was so fuckin' big, Belle! I just could not!" I whimpered. "And he was about to tear me to pieces! He warned me, but I wasn't ready! He went to get some ice down the hallway from our room when the white bitch came knocking at the door! Obviously, she can take dick! She's pregnant! She's been taking that dick for years! Might as well keep on taking it!"

Belle shook her head at my ignorance. "The only thing better than pussy to a nigga is some *new* pussy, silly rabbit. That nigga looks like he will teach, talk, and train you to do everything you need to do to please him. Shit, that bitch probably wouldn't or couldn't do. You know how to dance. And you can twerk better than half these strippers in here. Those ass cheeks of yours clap together when you walk, bitch. Clap them cheeks on that nigga's dick and stop playing. The bitch is probably lying about that baby. And even if she's not..." Belle sighed, watching me sit down on the bench. "Even if she's not lying, didn't you see the way that man looked at you at that courthouse today? He looked at you like he couldn't wait to spend the rest of his life with you. Like he wanted to unlearn all the shit he learned in that marriage to that bitch and relearn to love with you. I can't believe you put that fuckin' apron on top of those damn Pink pajamas! You are *not* coming back to work at the bar! Your nigga is flying you to Greece this weekend! You remember that shit? Don't fuck this up, please, bitch!"

I tightened my apron around my waist. "I'm not going back there. I don't give a fuck if you told Nate you were in a bind. Should've kept those tricks and treats to yourself, shit. Y'all planned this entire wedding ceremony before Jacyn even showed up at my grandma's house. The nigga dropped a tree on my Nana's house to get me to come back here! The house I'm putting up for sale so I can just move on with my life."

Belle shook her head, checking her body out as she sprayed on glittery body spray. "Well, how you gonna move on by coming back to your grandma's club, which is run by the woman who left you to die in filth!"

"I left my daughter to do what now?" Mama's voice bounced off the lockers of that dressing room.

Belle and I looked toward the doorway as Mama stepped into the room. The dancers scattered like roaches, hurrying to get it together and get back to the floor.

"Yeah, y'all better get it together. The horny niggas are out there, ready to see you hoes shake some ass. Whoever makes the least tonight is going home with that nigga out there who looks like the muthafucka who followed Diamond home to make sure she got home safe," Mama called out to the strippers as they scurried out of the dressing room. She shook her head, gripping a can of Lysol.

The last stripper who was making a run for it barely made it out the door before Mama was spraying in the air. She looked over at Belle, who was sitting on the bench beside me, buckling the straps to her stilettos. "Big Back, you need to tell your Stage Sistas to wash between their legs. Every time they leave the locker room, it smells like they forgot to take their pussy with them."

Belle smirked as she continued to buckle her shoes.

Mama walked toward us. She was wearing a short-sleeved, skin-tight body suit, a big red belt, and black patent leather Red Bottoms. Her dark hair was pulled up into a bun. Her bangs touched her thick, microbladed eyebrows. Her red-stained lips smacked together as she popped her chewing gum. "And speaking of pussy, why the fuck are you not at that hotel, giving yours to that gospel nigga?"

"See?" Belle mumbled under her breath.

I shook my head, my leg shaking anxiously. "It's not that simple, Mama."

"Did you think marrying a nigga you just met would be simple?" Mama scoffed, standing before me with her arms folded.

"Look, I'm not about to take marriage advice from a woman I've seen leave this club with a different nigga every fuckin' night." I huffed. "What the fuck do you know about marriage besides ruining one?"

Belle gasped, grabbing her things to hurry and put them in the locker. She hurried out of the room, leaving me to deal with my crazy mama on my own. Saying shit like that to my mother would usually get a bitch smacked. I wasn't just any bitch, though. I was the daughter she barely acknowledged.

Mama grinned a little, looking down into the tight frown on my face. "The nigga's wife came in here last Friday after the divorce. Told me she was pregnant. Said she was going to do whatever needed to be done to get her nigga back. Doesn't surprise me she'd show up to the hotel, moments after your wedding ceremony that I wasn't even invited to."

"I was invited last minute myself," I mumbled. "Everyone who should've been there was there."

"Do you love him?" Mama asked me.

I looked up at my mom, watching her check her pink stiletto nails. "I'm still trying to process him."

"Well, while you're over here trying to process your feelings for the nigga you married, your cousin is going to try and do whatever she can to interfere in your life. She had your father meet her here last Friday." Mama exhaled sharply as she watched my chest stop rising as my lungs took a quick pause.

"I came here to get my job back, not talk about that dysfunctional family. Grandma told me that my dad owns that fuckin casino in Concord, just eighteen minutes away, which is not that fuckin far from the Midnight Ballet. He knew I ran this place with my grandmother. Just like you knew where I was for eighteen years, I'm sure he knew, too."

Mama shook her head. "He didn't know until Scarlett told him about you. He didn't know about Jaliyah either, until she told him about Jaliyah being sent to a psychiatric facility. I left that man alone fifteen years ago, Melody. He had a better chance at a life with that bougie bitch Carolina McNealson."

I looked at my mother, shaking my head. The McNealson family was just as big in the gospel music industry as the Oxberrys. "Carolina McNealson, as in that gospel singer from Texas? Her daughter, Breelyn McNealson, has Grammy nominations! And she's only twenty-one!"

The light in Mama's eyes dimmed a little. "Breelyn's at the bar."

My eyes widened. "Why? Why is a gospel artist at the bar in a strip club?"

"She's here, visiting the Oxberry church. She's singing in the choir this weekend. She's in town to see her father. And here to meet her sister." Mama watched me slowly stand from the bench.

I shook my head. "Meet *what* fuckin' sister, Mama?"

"When I ran into your father at seventeen, he had a fiancée

and a five-year-old daughter. I didn't want to come between that," Mama tried telling me, but I wasn't trying to fuckin' hear that shit.

"See, what did I tell you? Fuckin' up marriages!" I laughed out loud, heading toward the door of the dressing room. "Another sister I haven't met, Mama? I'm sick of this fuckin' family and the secrets that fuckin' hurt!"

"Since you have an apron on, help Dreeka at the bar!" Mama called out as I let the door slam closed behind me.

I barely made it out the door before the tears came sliding down my face. I hadn't even gotten the chance to get to know my little sister when I was about to meet another sister. A sister who was known in the gospel industry. I only knew of her because of my grandmother's circle of friends. I guess Grandma did a lot of praying because she was trying to make up for all the sinning she was doing.

I dried my face as I walked down the hallway. Strippers pranced by, adjusting their bra tops and G-strings, greeting me as they passed. I entered the kitchen, bracing myself as I walked through the doorway leading into the bar. It didn't take long for me to spot Breelyn sitting at the end of the bar. She sipped from what looked like a Long Island Iced Tea as she eagerly looked around the bar, mesmerized by the asses shaking, money flying, and lights flickering. I slowly walked to the bar, eyes fixed on her.

"Boss's daughter." Dreeka's voice startled me on my left.

I didn't even look at her. My eyes were planted on Breelyn's pretty brown face. "What, Dreeka?" I huffed.

"Gospel nigga is here!" Dreeka tugged on my arm.

My heart jolted. I glanced to the left side of the bar, eyeing Jacyn. He gripped an empty glass in his hand, signaling one of the bartenders to come over and fix him another drink.

"He wants to talk to you." Dreeka let go of my arm and watched me nervously adjust my apron. "Bitch, are you wearing pajamas?"

"Well, I don't want to talk to *him*." I huffed, walking toward Breelyn. I'd deal with Jacyn later.

Breelyn caught sight of me as I walked in her direction. She smiled, deep dimples piercing her face. "Melody?" she questioned, making sure she'd matched my name with my face.

I sighed heavily as I approached her. "Unfortunately, that's me."

She nodded. "I've seen videos of you singing here on IG, YouTube, and TikTok! You've got skills!"

I rolled my eyes a little. "Vocal skills run in the Biggs family, I hear. They say our father can sing, too, though I've never met him to confirm it."

The smile on Breelyn's face dimmed. "He didn't know about you."

"Did you want me to fix you another drink or something? I've had a very bad day. I'm not really in the best mood for family reunions," I snapped.

"I came to invite you to church next Sunday if you're in town." Breelyn reached into her little Mark Jacobs bucket purse and pulled out a flyer. "We can catch up there. Maybe get some lunch. I'm moving here. I just bought a condo with my fiancé, and I'd love you to come over for my housewarming party. I wrote my number on the back of the flyer." She smiled again, even though I was frowning.

"Boss's daughter," Dreeka called out again, walking up to me with a Post-It note that time.

I huffed as Dreeka handed me the note that said, *Come here, mama*. I rolled my eyes, looking up into Dreeka's face as she giggled. "Dreeka, tell him to go play with his ex-wife and not me."

"He told me to tell you that if you didn't go over there, he was going to air this place out. He's on his third glass of Hennessy. He's been sitting there for about an hour while you were in the dressing room. I don't think he's playing. Kelsius, Marcellus, and Jacob just pulled up outside." Dreeka patted me on the shoulder before walking away, tossing a hand tower over her shoulder.

Breelyn glanced over at Jacyn before looking back at me. "You know the Oxberrys?"

I nodded. "I just married that one."

Breelyn's eyes widened as she sipped the last few drops of her drink. "Well," she put her glass down, "I should get out of here before I get too drunk to drive. If you know what's good for you, you'll do as your husband says." Sis giggled before getting up from her seat. "Don't be a stranger. Give me a call." She winked and placed a $20 tip down on the bar.

As she walked away from me, I called out to her. "I do have one question, though."

She stopped in her tracks before turning around, seemingly eager to answer my question. "Yeah?"

"What was it like having a father in your life?" I needed to know.

Breelyn shrugged. "I wouldn't know." And she walked away.

The night couldn't get any fuckin' worse. I watched as Breelyn walked away before I closed my eyes to take a deep breath, turning around to walk toward Jacyn. He sat at that bar, wearing the outfit he'd worn to our wedding ceremony. When I got closer to him, I noticed a rolled blunt in his left hand. Not only was he smoking, something I'd never seen him do, but he wasn't wearing his wedding ring. I don't know why that hurt when I'd given his rings back a few hours ago. But it did.

I cleared my throat once I got to him. "H-Hey," I stuttered, watching him exhale the thick, grayish smoke from his nose and mouth. It was then that I noticed the gold grill on the bottom row of Jacyn's mouth. When did the nigga get a fuckin' grill?

Jacyn looked up at me, his eyes low. "'Hey'? I am not your friend. You better greet me properly. Greet a nigga like we just said 'I do' today. Call a nigga 'daddy' or somethin'."

"Don't piss me the fuck off," I muttered.

"Don't *you* walk away from me. *Never* walk away from me when I'm fuckin' talking to you." Jacyn sounded like he was giving me a warning.

"Jacyn," I sighed heavily, coughing from the skunky smoke floating my way, "what are you doing here?"

"I told you I didn't want you working here anymore. Did you think I was playin' with you?" Jacyn questioned me. "You promised me for better or worse this afternoon at 3:17 p.m. We tied the fuckin' knot. This entanglement is forever. We were in the middle of exchanging souls. Let's go get back in bed."

I just watched him smoke. "You say that shit like your ex-wife didn't come to our hotel room! Did she tell you that her doctor screwed up her medical records?"

Jacyn nodded. "Yeah."

My heart was breaking all over again as I asked him, "Did she tell you she was having another one of your babies?"

Jacyn didn't answer that question. He just put the blunt to his lips and pulled from it. As he exhaled the vapors from his nose, he held up the blunt to pass it to me.

He was pissing me the fuck off, being way more nonchalant than usual. "I need some time to think. I think we need a break."

Jacyn's eyebrows lowered. "I think we don't need shit. Marriage doesn't work like this. Hang that apron up. Tell ya mama I hope she has insurance on this place because if I see you behind the bar again, I'm burning this place down, whether it's metaphorically speaking or physically."

"You already dropped a tree on Grandma's house. Now you wanna burn her legacy down?" I snapped.

"Fuck your grandma's house. Fuck her club. And fuck her." Jacyn said shit loud enough for the bottle girls who walked by to hear. They paused in their tracks to stand behind me, waiting for him to clean up his statement.

"Fuck my grandma?" I folded my arms.

"If you're asking if I respect a woman who's sold underage girls to men old enough to remember standing in line to drink from a water fountain that says 'coloreds', the answer is *fuck* her. If you're asking me if I respect a woman who had niggas killed in front of his wife and daughters, then punished the women even more by making their daughters sell pussy to pay back whatever their fathers owed her, then *fuck* her. While she was protecting her granddaughter, she was pimping out someone else's granddaughter. I did my homework on your 'grandmother'. Your mother bought this place with the money the Bigg's family gave her from pimping out young girls to those muthafuckas.

"Your mama runs this shit the way her mama did because your mama was one of those girls your grandma pimped the fuck out. This is all your mama knows. And I won't let this be all you know. You're never coming the fuck back here." Jacyn snarled at me, glancing at the bottle girls who stood behind me, ready to jump to my defense if they needed to. He put his blunt out in an ashtray that sat alongside his glass of Pure White Hennessy. "If you ladies want to make another dime in this muthafucka, you better tell your boss's daughter to hang that apron up, put my rings back on, and come get in this fuckin' car."

The bottle girls all hesitated, unsure what to say. They couldn't deny what he was saying. My grandmother kept me sheltered from a lot that was going on at the club. She kept me out of the dressing room with the strippers. She never let me see her books. She used code language when speaking to her employees. Even Belle didn't tell me half of the shit she'd do, afraid she'd lose her job. She'd been going to these "catering events" that Grandma had marked off on the calendar of events in her office. It wasn't until I was seventeen that I found out those events were swingers parties at undisclosed locations. And Belle had been the main attraction at every event since we were fifteen. My grandma killed a man and buried his remains under her patio to save my life. I couldn't hate her, even though I should have for what she did to her daughter. My mother, who couldn't love me or her younger daughter because all she knew was hate.

"Mellie!" Dreeka came running up to me. "Belle's in the back, throwing up!"

I hesitated, looking at Jacyn as he removed his gun from his pants and set it on his lap. I gulped, about to ask him what he planned to do with that shit, when Dreeka started yanking on my arm, pulling me away from the bar. There was no telling what Belle took. When she wanted to get high for whatever she was getting into for the night, she'd snort, smoke, or drink just about anything. I could hear Belle retching before we even hit the door to the dressing room. Two other strippers were holding Belle's wig back while she threw up in one of the trash cans.

"What the fuck did she take?" I asked loudly over the gut-wrenching sound.

"Just some coke, molly, and some lean. I think she might have popped a few percs earlier. Shit, your mama is sending her to some rapper's mansion tonight. No telling how much dick Belle was gonna have to take tonight!" Dominqua told me as she patted Belle's back.

I pulled my phone out of my pocket, about to dial 911.

Dreeka knocked my phone out of my hand. "Are you crazy? The last thing your mama wants is twelve out here!"

Belle pulled her head from the trash can long enough for me to see that she was coughing up blood from her nose and mouth. "I'm on stage next..." She barely got the words out of her mouth before she was hurling again.

"What the fuck is going on in here? DJ BlackAssNiggaWith-Waves just announced Big Back coming out center stage. Why is this bitch not center stage?" Mama's voice startled the strippers who were standing around, trying to help.

"Boss Lady, Belle is coughing up blood," Dreeka hesitated to say as everyone, but Belle turned to the sound of Mama's heels prancing across the dressing room floor.

"I don't give a fuck if she's coughing up dick," Mama growled, "it's her set. She wanted to make this money tonight to pay Miss Ethel's hospital bill."

I was confused. "Hospital bill?"

"Miss Ethel has an inoperable brain tumor. She's been in a coma for two weeks." Mama came over and eyed Belle vomiting in the trash can.

"I've been gone a month and a half." I ran my fingers through my hair. "Belle never mentioned her mama being in the hospital. And she paid for my hotel when she needed that money for her mama?" I looked back at Belle before I grabbed my phone from the floor where Dreeka had tossed it. "She needs a doctor! Call the paramedics!"

"She needs to get out there on stage. No one told her to take whatever she took. Aye, Belinda, Big Back, you need to get out there on that stage!" Mama went over and pulled Belle's head out of the trash can by her hair. Mama's eyes dimmed when she saw the blood running down Belle's face. "Dreeka, go get one of the security guards to carry her out of here. I'll have one of them take her to the hospital."

Dreeka didn't hesitate to do as she was told. She went running in her five-inch heels to get some help.

Mama pushed her bangs from her face, trying to remain calm. "Those rappers paid me fifty bands for you, Belle. *Fuck*! Someone needs to get on stage for her to at least make her payout for the night!"

"Hell nah. Kelsius's crew just strolled up in here. They'll be sitting first row, right by the stage. They will not fuck me raw tonight." Erotica scoffed, folding her arms. "Belle was dancing to 'Red Light Special' tonight, too, because her period just came on. She was letting these niggas know she was ready for them to speed through her shit."

I was sick to my fuckin' stomach listening to them having a fuckin' conversation about fuckin' strange niggas like the shit was normal. It was *their* normal, so they didn't see anything strange about fuckin' niggas they'd never met while on their period. I had no idea that my best friend's mama, who was my grandmother's best friend, was dying. Belle was so pressed about seeing me happy that she didn't let me see that she was in pain.

I got down on the floor with my best friend. "Oh, Belle..." I pushed her wild hair from her face.

"I-I can do it." Belle fell against me, blood and makeup

running down her face. "Your grandma used to come into this dressing room every night. She'd say," she laughed and coughed at the same time, "she'd say, 'I'm going to tell my hoes like I told my daughter: you better get out there and suck some dick!'"

I looked down at Belle as she laughed, high out of her mind, then I looked up at the horrified look on my mother's face. It was more like the look of a person who was instantly taken back to the most painful part of their life.

I didn't know what else to say to make that hurt expression on my mother's go away, except, "Mama, she doesn't know what she's saying."

Mama's hurt expression instantly changed to anger, the only emotion I'd seen my mother revert to in the three years that I'd known her. "Someone better get the fuck on that stage for her tonight, or I'm firing this bitch."

Erotica and Dominiqua both looked at me.

"Shit, Mellie should go out there. The audience loves this bitch's voice. You wanna entertain the niggas in VIP tonight, Boss Lady? Put your daughter on the floor. Security won't let anyone touch her. You know they'll guard her with their lives," Erotica suggested.

Dominiqua wasn't so sure. "Didn't she just marry one of the Oxberry brothers? They're out there tonight!"

Mama looked me over, skeptical at first, until the bitches kept on talking.

"Announce her, Miss Dawnna. Tell the niggas if they wanna see the Club Virgin in a thong, they gotta throw, let's say, a total of $5000 on stage. Once they start flicking hundreds, fifties, twenties and shit, send her ass out there on stage. Then, if they want the bitch to take something off, they gotta toss more money on stage. Then, if they want her in VIP, they gotta toss some more. She'll make Belle's payout and a few dollars back from what you promised those rappers tonight. They're gonna want your best stripper at that party tonight." Erotica nodded her head toward me.

Mama shook her head as security came into the dressing room to peel Belle off the floor. "I'm not sending my fuckin' daughter to that party tonight. I'll send a few of you hoes over there, but not my daughter. It's her honeymoon."

I looked up at Adam, my grandma's favorite security guard, as he pulled Belle away from me. Grandma used to fuck the shit out the nigga to get him to follow me around for her to make sure I stayed out of trouble. He picked me up from school. He even had his younger cousin beating niggas up at school for trying to talk to me. My grandmother was so determined to make sure I didn't turn out like any of the women she'd pimped out, my mother included.

Adam carried my friend out of the room as Dreeka came back in, looking flustered as ever, like she just crawled her way out of a fight. "Ms. Dawnna, baby, those niggas out there are drunk and fighting over the strippers. If you don't get someone out there to distract them muthafuckas, they're about to fuck the club up!"

Mama, Erotica, and Dominqua all looked at me like I was their only help that night.

"You better get out there like you're Mercedes, and you're doing your last dance!" Erotica went over to her locker to grab me an outfit.

Erotica looked scared for me. "Shit, I have a feeling this is gonna be her first *and* last dance. A quick dance at that."

I hadn't known my mama that long, but what I did know about her was that she loved money. Nothing mattered more to her than money. The moment Belle got out of the hospital, my mama was going to sell every inch of that girl's body to get back the money she'd lost. She was going to send every stripper willing to open their legs that night to meet those rappers who booked Belle. And if I didn't take the stage in place of Belle that night, mama was going to fire Belle after she got her money's worth out of my friend.

Erotica helped me into my outfit that night. We stood in the hallway that led out onto the stage as she pulled the straps on my bra top to tighten them. I'd taken a shower in the locker room before slipping into a ruby red sequined bra top that didn't cover anything but my nipples and a red sequined thong. I had the keys to Belle's locker. She was gonna kill me when she found out I wore her favorite red Giuseppe Harmony Love stilettos. Those heels dropped in the year of 2018. Couldn't find those shoes anymore. Her mother gave them to her on her sixteenth birthday five years ago. She only brought those out on occasions when she felt she needed all the luck she could get. And that night, as DJ BlackAssNiggaWithWaves announced my name while playing the instrumental to "Nasty Song," *I* was the one needing all the luck that I could get.

Dreeka brushed my hair, while Dominiqua nervously tamed my edges. Regina was kneeling on the floor, rubbing my legs down with golden hour cocoa butter oil. I felt like I was auditioning to work at Pussy Valley. Mama stood against the hallway wall, pretending not to be nervous as she smoked her casino flavored Black-N-Mild.

"I know y'all niggas wanna see The Virgin shake some ass, don't ya?" DJ BlackAssNiggaWithWaves hyped the crowd.

My grandma let the guests know not to fuck with me years ago when she put my name as The Virgin Assistant Manager on a plaque hanging outside the club. Muthafuckas would come to the bar, asking for me, The Virgin, to make them a Virgin Mellie, which was the Sunday drink special. The fake ass pastors and deacons would come to the club that night to see me shake some ass while I made their drinks. That's all they'd get out of me, fully dressed except maybe some booty shorts every now and then. Until that night, I'd never been on stage. I had to keep telling myself it was to keep my best friend employed. To keep her mama alive a little longer.

Regina got off the floor and handed me my sequined microphone that I kept behind the bar. "Take one for the team, baby."

"I'm not taking shit," I mumbled, nervous out of my mind as the intro to "Red Light Special" played over the loud speakers.

"If you want The Virgin to come out, y'all better start throwing them hundreds, fifties and twenties on the stage, muthafuckas. Rent is due, the light bill is high, and food is fuckin' expensive. Throw that shit!" the DJ shouted as cheers filtered the air. "She's not coming out until the stage looks like leaves piled up on my muthafuckin lawn that I need to rake! Let me see them Franklins, Grants and Jacksons falling, or The Virgin not shaking shit for you niggas!"

Mama stood up from leaning against the wall to go stand close to the squinted curtain that blocked the entrance to the stage. She exhaled deeply as she peeped through the gap in the curtain. "You're saving that junkie bitch's job tonight." Mama pulled from her Black.

Mama's strippers glanced at me as soon as that remark left mama's lips.

"That junkie bitch is only a junkie bitch to survive the nights she's worked at this fuckin club." I shoved the strippers away from me as I approached the curtain. "After you make your money tonight, you may never see either of us again. So, I hope you enjoy the show."

Mama looked at me as I stood at the other end of the doorway. "The only thing keeping these niggas from touching you is me. If I turn on that flashing green light during your performance, one of these niggas has the opportunity to snatch you off stage and take you home with him tonight and do whatever he wants to you for four hours. You'll need some blow, too, after they rip you a new pussy, little virgin. So, I'd watch your mouth if I were you. I'm just asking you to dance for the night, but if I want you to use that mouth for something other than talking shit to your mother, I can and I will."

"Mellie, just-just chill." Dreeka tried to warn me, her voice shaky.

"Mama, I will have this entire club shutdown. I don't give a fuck if half of the Mecklenburg police department are paying customers. Those niggas have wives. Wives who would love to fuck your world up for fuckin' with theirs. You've ruined my life enough! Watch me ruin yours if you touch any of that money flying out there. I'm doing this for Belle, not you, a mother who's done absolutely nothing for me but remind me of who I never the fuck *ever* want to be!"

Mama just looked at me, her chest heaving as the deejay announced that it was showtime. "Oh, you really wanna play with Mama tonight?" She grinned a little. "I sure hope ya husband can shoot back."

The instrumental started over, and I glared at my mother as I turned on the microphone before placing it to my lips. "Take a good look at it, look at it now..." I pushed the curtain back as I stepped through the doorway.

Whistles and yells dominoed throughout the club as I was damn near blinded by all the lights. Strippers were sliding down the three poles on that stage as I strolled down the middle. My blurred vision cleared as I passed by the moving spotlights. I looked toward the entrance to the dance floor, eying Scarlett and Bonnie standing there, looking like the fuckin' twins from *The Shining*.

"Don't go too fast, don't go too slow, you gotta let your body flow..." I sang, eyeing the men at the front of the stage.

Security lined the stage so the men couldn't get close enough to touch us. But then something happened. It appeared as though all six security guards got a text. They pulled out their phones and looked at them before looking at each other. And then they stepped away from the stage. I looked up at Adam who stood alongside the head of security, Larry, at the bar. They, too, got a text before looking at each other. The crowd had already moved closer to the stage and made it damn near impossible for Adam or Larry to move through the crowd should anything pop off that night.

I continued to sing as money flew onto the stage. Bills were everywhere. I definitely felt like I was walking through a yard covered in leaves as I strutted across the stage. "Baby, it's yours, all yours, if you want it tonight..."

I don't think I even got the lyrics to the chorus out completely when the spotlights that were just flashing red, immediately turned green and stopped moving, shining directly on me. Peeping over my shoulder, I caught sight of the strippers who were once swirling around the poll immediately slide down and onto the floor. Mama's silhouette lurked behind the curtain. Her devilish laughter was heard before her shadowy figure disappeared. I looked back out at the crowd, about to step back from the front of the stage when one of the muthafuckas at the front grabbed me by my ankle.

"Come here, bitch!" he growled at me.

Trying to pull away from him, I fell back onto the floor. The nigga dragged me by both ankles, trying to yank me off the stage. Just as the strippers on stage ran toward me to pull my arms back in the opposite direction, gunshots rang out. A bullet went straight through the left side of that nigga's head, and he dropped to the floor. The strippers ducked, and all hell broke loose.

I looked toward the deejay booth, where the shots came from. Jacyn stood there, blunt to his lips, gripping his gun at his side. I looked back down at the nigga bleeding out on the floor. Whoever was with the nigga reached in his pocket, probably reaching for his phone because the regular muthafuckas definitely weren't getting in with a gun. The only ones who were allowed in the club with a gun were the VIP guests who were usually less thirsty and chillin' at the bar or in VIP. Reaching for his phone, when he should've been running like Forrest Gump with everyone else, was a mistake. The moment he reached in his pocket, he was shot in his hand and his hip. Those shots came from above, in VIP. I looked up to see Kelsius standing behind the guardrails, looking out over the crowd at anyone who was reaching for a phone instead of running out of the club.

"My bullets move fast. Y'all niggas too slow!" Kelsius sang to the tune of the song, laughing as he watched me stumbling, trying to get off the floor. I was so scared that my legs buckled under me.

When the strippers realized we weren't the ones being targeted, they rushed over to help me off the floor. As we attempted to get off the stage, Jacyn called out to me over the microphone.

"Now, come get your ass in the fuckin' car, Melody Oxberry. My mama wants us at the fuckin' church." Jacyn snarled before dropping the microphone.

CHAPTER 4
Melody

"Belle needed the money." I stood outside the club, watching as police cars darted into the parking lot, seven deep. Typical night at the club. Bullets flying, nobody sees nothing, a dead body or two, blood for the strippers to scrub off the floor because my bitch ass mama wasn't ruining her $150 powder nails.

Jacyn and I stood alongside his brother, Jacob's burgundy Maserati. The guns used in the shooting were gotten rid of by Blackie and Queen City Girl, the two strippers who helped me off stage that night. As soon as those green lights came on, they knew what was going on. They knew Mama was setting me up to get fucked. They never liked my mama and only worked there to pay their way through nursing school.

Jacyn removed his jacket, wrapping it around my shoulders. "It's belt to ass about these little feelings I have left, Melody." Jacyn's nostrils flared.

"You're calm. I should've known there was a storm inside you. You didn't have to kill him." I glanced at the police walking inside the club.

"Would you rather I kill your mother? The woman who gave niggas the go to grab what's mine? Because that was my first instinct. If she had been standing next to him at the foot of that stage, it would've been her brains splattered instead of his. She's not the reason your friend is at that hospital. Belle is not your responsibility. Her debt isn't yours. I can pay for my own fuckin' hotel room. I can pay her the money back, but I can't give her dignity back for whatever she did to get that money. And neither can you." Jacyn told me, grabbing my body to his by his jacket that was draped around me.

"I don't want her coming back here," I whispered to him.

"You just make sure I don't see your ass back here," Jacyn warned me.

I looked over his shoulder to see Bonnie and Scarlett coming out of the club with one of the officers. My eyes widened, wondering if the bitch was telling the cops that Jacyn and Kelsius were responsible for the shooting. When I saw the cop walk toward his car instead of in our direction, I could breathe somewhat normally. They told the cops something, and it was probably something that could get the club shut down. Just when I thought the night couldn't get any worse, the bitches were walking in our direction.

I looked back at Jacyn. "Your ex-wife is coming this way."

"I don't have a fuckin' ex-wife." Jacyn looked down into my face, not even looking in the direction of the footsteps approaching him.

"Cyn," Scarlett called Jacyn by his nickname as she approached us with the bitch I was going to smack dead in her mouth if she said anything to me. "That was quite a show you and Kelsius put on for everyone."

I clinched my teeth as Scarlett stood before us, tightening her Burberry trench coat around her waist.

Jacyn looked from me to Scarlett. "If you liked the show, you'll definitely enjoy the after party if you say anything to my wife. They'll be two funerals this week instead of one." Jacyn looked over Scarlett's shoulder as paramedics wheeled the man Kelsius shot out of the club on a gurney.

"Cyn," Scarlett drew Jacyn's attention back to her, "this baby needs you to be Jacyn."

Jacyn's temples twitched. "Jacyn needed you to be a fuckin' wife. Cyn doesn't give a fuck what the baby that you don't even want needs. I suggest you walk the fuck away from me."

Bonnie huffed, about to say something when Jacob rolled his window down.

"Bro, get the fuck in the car." Jacob started the engine.

Scarlett glanced at me before digging her hands in her pocket to remove to bottles of pills. "Take this one in the morning with eight ounces of water and this—" She jumped as Jacyn snatched the bottles from her. She giggled a little before looking at me. "If you want Jacyn back, make him take those pills. Otherwise—"

Jacyn reached in his pants for the second gun he had on him.

I gasped when Kelsius got out of the front passenger seat.

"Nigga, get the fuck in the car. Scarlett, Bonnie, get the fuck out of here." Kelsius walked around the car to us and stood between his brother and Scarlett. He faced Jacyn, who seemed to be looking straight through him. "Bro, get in the car. Fuck Scarlett. Let's go home. We came here to get Jacyn's wife, remember?"

Why were they talking about Jacyn like he wasn't standing right there? I had questions, so many questions.

Jacyn looked at Kelsius, the angry expression on his face changing to an expression of confusion. Like he was trying to register the events that had just happened. "Jacyn's wife? I have their rings in my pocket."

Kelsius nodded. "Yes. Get in the backseat and put these rings on her finger. Shawty's dress is in the car. She can change at my place before heading over to the church."

Jacyn frowned again, hand back on his gun. "Nigga, she doesn't belong to you."

"Or she can walk into the church wearing a thong if that makes sense to you. Shit, I'm trying to help," Kelsius assured his brother, taking the pill bottles from his hand. "Get in the car." He moved his brother aside, so he could open the back door.

"Cyn, we need to talk." Scarlett watched as Jacyn grabbed me by the hand before getting inside the car, pulling me along with him.

I got in the car, and Kelsius shut the door behind me. I could hear Bonnie cursing him the fuck out as he walked around the car to get in the front passenger seat. Kelsius barely got his foot in the car before Jacob was balling out of the parking lot.

"Bitch!" Kelsius yelled at his adoptive brother. "Can I get my fuckin' feet in this muthafucka? You're balling the fuck out of the parking lot like we didn't just shoot two muthafuckas, like Twelve isn't still in the fuckin' parking lot."

Jacob glanced at Kelsius, clicking his teeth. "Man, I was supposed to pull up at Dreeka's spot tonight. Y'all two niggas fucked it up over this bi—"

In seconds, the barrel of Jacyn's gun was in Jacob's neck. "This *what*, nigga? Repeat what you said a little louder, so I can blow your fuckin' tongue off."

"Kelsius, if your brother gets blood on my new seats, I'm gonna come back and haunt both you muthafuckas." Jacob chuckled.

Kelius turned around in his seat, bottle of Gatorade alkaline in his hand. "Cyn, pop open that bottle of hydroxyzine. Take out two of the pills."

"I don't need no fuckin' pills. I need you muthafuckas to respect his wife whether she's in Jacyn's presence or by herself. Don't touch her. Don't look at her too long. And don't let anything happen to her when Jacyn can't be there. You better be on your best fuckin' behavior when addressing her. Do you fuckin' feel me?" Jacyn mushed Jacob in the back of his head before sitting back in his seat.

Kelsius quickly unscrewed one of the bottles. "Man, when is the last time you took your fuckin' meds, Cyn? You need these!"

I looked at Jacyn as he gripped the gun in his hand, rocking against the leather seats, agitation taking over his body. I should have been afraid to grab his hand, but I wasn't. I lightly placed my hand over his before gripping it in mine.

Jacyn looked down at my hand and opened his, allowing me to intertwine my fingers with his. "You left him," Jacyn said softly yet sternly.

"I'm sorry." I admitted that I was wrong to leave him instead of making Scarlett's stupid ass get the fuck out of our room.

Kelsius handed me the water bottle.

I took the water bottle from Kelsius and pressed it against Jacyn's chest.

Jacyn hesitated, letting go of his gun to take the water bottle from my hand.

Kelsius handed two white pills to me, and I put them to Jacyn's lips. "This is his PRN. He takes these twice a day, every day, Melody. Make sure he takes these, alright?"

My heart was pounding in my chest, even though I was playing it cool on the outside. "Take them, Cyn. Please, for me."

Jacyn frowned at me but opened his mouth to let me slide the pills through his lips. Then, he took a few gulps of water.

"Show Jacyn's wife that you took those pills," Kelsius demanded.

Jacyn looked me in the face as he opened his mouth, moving his tongue up and down and around, showing me that he wasn't hiding the pills in his cheeks.

Kelsius sighed deeply before he turned around in his seat and sat back, slumping down, scratching his head anxiously. "You gotta calm down before we get back to Lydia's place. She wants us there for dinner. Then, y'all two can finish whatever freaky shit you started in that hotel room. And then fly the fuck out to Greece to get away from muthafuckin' Charlotte before Scarlett starts her bullshit. Nigga, you got that hoe pregnant?"

Jacob glanced at Kelsius before looking at me through the rearview mirror. The look in his eyes, I'd seen it before. Someone who had secrets. Secrets that could turn lives upside down. He looked away from me and back at the road.

"H-how long will it take him to get back to himself?" I asked, looking back at Jacyn as I slouched down in the leather seat.

"It'll take about thirty minutes to calm him down when he gets like this. Been a minute since he's had one of these episodes. I don't know what made him stop taking his meds. He takes Seroquel and Abilify. They took him off the Thorazine a few months back," Kelsius answered.

"What is this? What's happening to him? Why isn't he Jacyn?" I needed to know about the man that I married.

"Dissociative Identity Disorder," Jacob spoke up. "When he calms down enough to remember his name is Jacyn, he probably won't even remember what happened tonight. Any of it. Lucky if he remembers marrying you this afternoon."

That thought scared me. "Where did he put our rings?" I asked.

"Check his pockets." Kelsius glanced back at me over his shoulder.

I attempted to let go of his hand, but he gripped my hand tightly. So, I used my left hand to reach into both of his pants pockets until I found our rings. "Cyn, baby, you have to let go of my hand, so I can slide our rings on," I whispered to him, my eyes tracing his profile as he looked straight ahead.

Jacyn loosened his grip on my hand.

I grabbed his left hand and slid his wedding band onto his finger. Then, I placed my rings in his hand. "Remember what you told me this afternoon? You told me, 'On this day, I give you all of me in exchange for all of you.' You told me that I was every prayer you prayed, every laugh you laughed, every—"

"Every song I sang. Every promise I made," Jacyn finished my sentence.

"See? He remembers," I told his brothers as I watched Jacyn slide my rings onto my left finger.

"Aye, sis," Kelsius called out to me, "remember when I left your ass in that hotel?"

Jacyn grabbed his gun as both of his brothers started laughing.

"Yeah, it's starting to come back. Welcome back, bro." Kelsius's laugh subsided before he looked at me over his shoulder. "But seriously, sis, you remember?"

I rolled my eyes from Jacyn still gripping his gun to Kelsius' face. My irritated expression subsided when I realized he was asking me a serious question. "Yes, I remember."

"I bet you're glad it didn't work out, huh?" He grinned before his smile faded, and he looked straight again. "I know I am. My brother back there needs a woman like you. A woman who sees his other side and stays, only a few days into getting to know him. You have the option to leave. You'd already taken the rings off and gave them back to a nigga. And after seeing my brother breaking down, you don't seem afraid. Good ass woman, that's what you are. Just what that nigga needs. Fuck Scarlett. Fuck that baby, too."

I looked up to see Jacob looking right back at me. There was something about that nigga I didn't like at all.

* * *

By the time we got to The Oxberry Church of Saints, Jacyn was completely quiet. Kelsius got out of the car and headed inside the church. Jacob went in his truck to grab the original boxes that I'd opened that morning, which contained the dress and shoes that Jacyn showed up with at my grandmother's house. That I'd married him in that day. That he'd taken off that afternoon that was supposed to be my first time with him. With anyone.

Jacob tapped on the window to get his brother to roll it down. Once Jacyn rolled down his window, Jacob handed him the boxes. "Change in the car," he told me. "Don't fuck up my seats, trying to do something to calm this nigga's nerves. And don't come in my mama's church looking like your mama owns a whore house, ya know, even if she does." Jacob smirked, barely finishing his sentence before Jacyn was rolling the tinted window back up. "Muhfucka, don't run all my gas out!"

"Nigga talks too much," Jacyn snarled, after not saying a word the entire forty-five minutes it took us to get across town in that Monday Charlotte traffic. There was never a time of day when traffic wasn't bumper-to-bumper, even at 11:00 at night. 11:00, and his mom wanting us to meet up at the church for dinner was insane.

"11:00 dinner is crazy, Jacyn," I spoke up, watching him reach over the front seats to place the boxes.

"She probably just finished choir practice," Jacyn recalled.

That was good. He was calm enough to come back to reality for the moment. He was responding to his name instead of looking at me crazy for addressing him as Jacyn.

"The aunties in the choir always cook a big meal after they sing for four hours. When Jacob opened his mouth and told Mama I gave my last name to you in the courthouse today, Mama told me that I had to bring you over." Jacyn leaned back in his seat.

"D0…" I hesitated to ask him about what happened at the club. "Do you remember what happened tonight at the club?"

Jacyn leaned his head against the head rest. "Bits and pieces," he admitted. "I remember you walking out of the hotel room after whatever conversation you had with Scarlett. After that, everything else is a blur. I do remember seeing you walk out onto a stage in that outfit you're wearing now. Someone grabbed you, didn't they?"

I hesitated to nod, watching Jacyn pat his pants down for his other gun. "A few of Mama's strippers got rid of the guns involved. Bonnie and Scarlett were at the club tonight. Scarlett handed Kelsius these pill bottles for you to take. You took two pills to calm you down. I think she gave him a bottle of hydroxyzine and a bottle of Seroquel. I guess you already have the other bottle at the hotel or something."

"I won't be Jacyn all the time if that's alright with you." Jacyn turned his head to look at my face, as if he was expecting me to have a repulsed reaction.

I shrugged. "I'm not myself all of the time either."

"Yeah, but when I'm the other me, I'm not like me, if that makes sense. I struggle without those meds." Jacyn exhaled sharply.

"Then why haven't you been taking them?" I asked.

"Cyn doesn't like them because he can't come out to play as much. He wanted to play with you, too, on our honeymoon. He wanted to be able to talk to you. So, I stopped taking the pills on Friday," Jacyn told me.

"The day you had a tree dropped on Nana's house? Gotcha. Makes sense. Or was that Cyn?" I asked.

"You making fun of me, nigga?" Jacyn sat up in his seat.

I shook my head, disagreeing with his accusations. "I don't make fun of someone's pain."

"I'm not in pain when I'm Cyn. Cyn met you that night at the club. We were both there that night. I didn't take my meds, so I could watch those documentaries about Hurricane Katrina and not feel a thing. When I'm Cyn, I don't see my mama's bloated body floating in that water. In Cyn's world, Mama's still here. In Cyn's world, he saved her, and she's at home, watching those corny Lifetime movies." Jacyn laughed to himself, leaning back in his seat.

I removed his jacket from my shoulders and tossed it over the back of the chair.

Jacyn glanced at my outfit. His jaws tightened as he pulled that gun out of his pants and set it on the floor. "You said you were dancing for Belle. Said she needed the money," he recalled.

I didn't want to think about Belle. On the ride over, Jacob mentioned stopping by the hospital to check on her. I was her in-case-of-emergency person and hadn't received any calls from the hospital, saying she was crashing. So, I guess that was good news.

"Yeah. Her mama is dying, and she didn't even tell me. She'd been helping me lay low for over a month and never mentioned her mama. But that's Belle—always pretending like everything is okay." I looked at Jacyn, his eyebrows crinkled as if he was recalling more events from that night.

"Green lights at the club mean 'go'," Jacyn hissed. "Ya mama turned on her green lights when you sang to the audience tonight. Am I remembering that right?"

"No," I mumbled.

"Cyn wanted to kill her, but she wasn't out on the dance floor." Jacyn grabbed my leg, putting my thigh over his, and he started unbuckling the shoes I had on. "Kelsius texted Cyn that you were wearing the shoes that Belle was going to wear tonight to go fuck about eight niggas at a rapper's birthday party. I don't give a fuck what your friend does, you are not her. You will never be her. You will never do the things she does for money. I would never put you in the position to even think you had to do that shit to survive. You put yourself in danger to save her, and that won't happen again. If you can't convince her to leave that club, let her go. You hear me? Let her go."

I watched him unbuckle my shoes. "You killed that nigga."

"And it felt good to do it. I felt it when Cyn pulled that trigger. We were one in that moment, and the shit felt good to be whole. The only time I feel whole is when I'm with you. Tonight is proof that you let me be me, even when I'm not me." Jacyn reached for my other thigh, pulling that one over his as well. "Did you want that nigga grabbing on you?"

I shook my head. "No, of course not."

"And that's why he's gone. Whatever you face has to face *me*." Jacyn assured me. "Both of me."

I turned to him as he removed the other shoe. "Scarlett knows who you are. She wanted to bring you what you needed."

Jacyn disagreed. "Nah, she wanted to see what you would do when you found out your husband is a psychiatrist and a mental patient all in one. You left me when you found out about the baby; she figured you'd leave again after finding out my diagnosis. Are you leaving me?"

"I'm twenty-one, Jacyn. I haven't even lived yet," I told him.

Jacyn frowned, unbuckling my heel and letting it fall to the spotless floor. "You can live with me."

"I don't wanna deal with her. She's my cousin but she's not family. I can't coparent with that bitch. And as a wife, I should be able to do that. This is all new to me. I can love Joel; he was here before me. But to watch Scarlett use this baby to come around you, I don't know if I can handle that. I'm just learning you. That's going to be a journey in itself. I don't want to learn her. What she's teaching me right now is that she's going to be a problem." I wanted to cry thinking about it. "When I thought the bitch was dying, I knew I wouldn't have to deal with her anymore. You saw the results; this bitch will probably outlive us all! You know demons have better luck than angels! I planned to sell my grandma's house and move far, far the fuck away from here."

"I can't live without you." Jacyn tugged at the string to my thong, loosening it.

"You-you just met me." I sighed, heaving as I watched the bow come undone on one side before he reached around me to untie the other.

"Doesn't feel like we just met. Feels like I knew you in another lifetime. A better lifetime." Jacyn pulled my body onto his, looking up at me as I straddled him.

"I don't even know if I want children," I let him know.

Jacyn shrugged. "We don't have to make that decision today." He reached for his belt, pulling it from the buckle.

"She wants you back." I looked down as he unhooked his pants before unzipping them. "Don't you miss her? I know you didn't stop loving her."

Jacyn frowned up at me. "The moment I met you, I started questioning if I ever loved her in the first place."

I was too afraid to look down as I felt him reaching into his pants to pull that fuckin' horse from the stable again. "Jacyn—"

"Now, we're gonna try this shit again. If you don't like it, we will take things from there, aight?" Jacyn reached around my neck to untie my bra.

I lifted my hair from my shoulders as he pulled my bra from my body. I didn't even have time to lock my knees against his waist before he was guiding his dick through my pussy lips to find the opening.

"Inhale..." he coached my breathing.

I took a deep breath in.

"Now, let that shit out." He found the opening, digging his way through me.

And I let out an, "Oh, fuckin' shit!" My knees locked against him.

He held my hips, pressing my body down onto him so he could rest deep inside of me. "How does that shit feel? Does it feel like it wants that bitch back? Huh? Look at me when I'm fuckin talking to you, sexy-ass woman. Look at daddy when I'm asking you a question."

I moaned, looking down at him, frantically shaking my head. "Is he really mine?"

"I signed him over to you today. He's not going anywhere." Jacyn moaned as his dick throbbed inside me. "Reach behind you and dig in my left jacket pocket."

Jacyn sat up so I could each for his jacket pocket. I dug inside, anxiously pulling out what looked like a pink diamond necklace at first. Jacyn took the necklace from my hand and dropped it to reveal its length. I watched him slip the necklace through one of the heart rings before he put it around my neck. The moment I pulled my hair from the necklace, Jacyn pulled on one of the hearts, and he pulled on the diamond studded chain until the necklace wrapped snuggly around my neck. I was terrified.

Jacyn leaned back, and the necklace got tighter. When I reached for my neck to loosen it, he snatched my hand away. "What's my fuckin' name?" His voice was a familiar tone. The tone he had at the club when he was no longer Jacyn.

"C-Cyn." I knew who he was.

"Nah, pretty baby. What's my muthafuckin' name?" Jacyn tugged tighter until I was gasping for air. "It starts with a fuckin' D." He loosened the chain enough for me to gasp and breathe for air.

"Daddy!" I yelped.

"Ride this dick like I'm fuckin daddy, then. Fuck me before I fuck you, Mrs. Oxberry." Jacyn said that shit like he was fuckin' another man's wife.

I shouldn't have hesitated, because he sure as fuck didn't. He wrapped his arm around my waist and started pumping from the bottom. Not too hard, not too soft, but at the perfect pace and tempo. And he tugged at that chain with his other hand. He was making sure I couldn't run. Making sure I wasn't going anywhere. Making sure I felt every bit of him.

I reached for his pants legs, pushing them down further. The pressure around my neck was nothing compared to the pressure I felt as he ground into my walls. To relieve some of that pressure from inside, I started to grind with him. Grind and bounce to control his tempo.

"Shit. Fuck." Jacyn loosened his grip on that chain a little. "I'm sorry. That wasn't me."

"He can fuck me, too, if he wants," I leaned over and whispered in his ear. "You can both fuck me. Did Scarlett let the two of you fuck her?"

Jacyn looked into my face as I looked down at him. "You don't want that. Not yet."

I pulled myself off him, both of us looking down at the clear coat that I left on his dick. As I got off his lap, he kicked his pants off. And I turned around, bending over. I slid off the back seat a little so that one leg was resting on the floor and the other was resting on the backseat. Ass in the air. Pussy opening like a flower, so he could see how pink she was.

"Pretty ass pussy," Jacyn growled. "Pretty asshole. Every one of your holes is mine tonight, baby. Do you hear me? Starting here in the car and ending up back at the hotel." He slipped his fingers through my pussy lips, massaging her, patting her, rubbing her.

That shit didn't do anything but make me arch further. I was so afraid yet turned on at the same time. There we were, fuckin' on church grounds. His brothers knew what the fuck was going to happen when they left us alone in that car.

Jacyn reached for my neck, adjusting the chain so he could grab the loose end. With his other hand, he put himself back inside me, that time, digging so deep that it caused me to let go of the arch I once held.

Jacyn instantly wrapped that chain around his fist, yanking on it, causing me to throw my head back and look up at him. "If I told you to give me this muthafuckin' pretty pussy, why the fuck are you running from this dick?"

"You're-you're going to hurt me," I panted.

"If I hurt you, Jacyn will heal you. When you want love, you call on that nigga. When you want to be fucked, you call on me. Balance, mama. Now, show me that fuckin' arch. The more you run, the deeper I'm going to go. So, hold still until I tell you to fuck back. Yeah, don't you move. Hold it just like that, yeah. This is *my* pussy. I licked it, so it's mine, right? Don't play with me," Jacyn warned, pulling my body back to his.

Why the fuck would I even get into that position with a man who had a dick like a fuckin' eighteen-wheeler? As soon as I put that arch in my back, Jacyn started going in, immediately causing my fuckin' toes to curl. The moment I attempted to shorten my arch, Jacyn was pulling on that choker.

"You left a nigga after you promised him forever." Jacyn started pumping faster, my ass smacking against his pelvis. "Then, you were wearing this fuckin' floss with glitter on it in front of all them niggas at the club Jacyn told you he didn't want you to go back to. Bad girl." The nigga had me by the choker *and* my hair at that point. He was digging into me like a spade when a gardener is trying to loosen the soil, lifting and turning it to break up the clumps.

"I can be good!" I squealed grabbing onto the seat with one hand, and the other hand grabbing the diamond-stitched floor mat. "Daddy, I'll be good!"

"Throw that ass back on me. Grind with a nigga. Slow. Just like that. Give Daddy that pretty pussy." Jacyn glanced at me as I looked back at him. Then, he looked down at me popping my ass back on him and throwing it in a slow, steady circle. "Fucckkk... look at that wet pussy sliding up and down on this dick. Throw that shit back. Faster. Harder. Oouuu, that pussy creaming and squirting on that dick."

I moaned, feeling like I was peeing as I smacked my ass against him. That shit hurt so good. I gasped for air as he let go of my hair and the chain, grabbing my hips and throwing my pussy onto him. I squealed as Jacyn put his foot up onto the back seat and dug into me, balls deep. His balls clapped against my asshole as he pulled my body against his to the rhythm of his stroke. I felt like I was going to fuckin' explode.

"Jacyn, baby, it hurts!" I cried out.

Instantly, Jacyn lowered his leg, bringing his foot down from the back seat. His body hovered over mine, his chest pressing against my back. I could feel his heart beating rapidly as he intertwined his fingers with mine, grabbing onto the backseat together.

"Did Cyn hurt you?" Jacyn whispered in my ear as he slowed his stroke but still ground into me with the same tempo that his alternate moved.

"Yes..." I whined. "Baby, it hurts... it hurts so good."

"Your pussy feels so warm. And tight. I wanna cum in my wife. Can I fill this pussy up?" Jacyn kissed my neck, pausing in the pussy to savor the moment.

"I'm not on birth control. Cyn, I don't want a baby right now." I exhaled sharply, realizing I'd slipped up and called out a name I shouldn't have, at a moment when Jacyn was ready to put his kids in me. Without medication, I would have to learn to deal with the two of them simultaneously. I didn't know his med schedule. I didn't know if he even planned to continue taking them, but I did know, that for whatever reason, both of him came whenever I called.

Jacyn let go of my hand and grabbed my waist, pulling my body into his as he dug into me. The more I moaned and screamed in blissful agony, the deeper he dug. "Give me that muthafucka. Take this dick. Cum on this dick. This is your dick. Keep taking it like it's yours. If I wanna cum in this pussy, I'ma cum in this pussy. Do you fuckin' hear me?"

Though I wanted that nigga to pull out of me, the moment I felt his dick start to throb, I threw that pussy back on him, grinding with him until he exploded inside me. Though he filled me like a Twinkie, he was still hard. When I thought he would keep going, he pulled out of me and dragged my body all the way onto the leather seats. The moment he turned my body over, he pulled my pussy towards his face, gripping my thighs in his hands.

His semen slid down my thighs the moment he turned me over. I looked down at him, and he looked up at me as he kissed every inch of my pussy like he was kissing the lips on my face. Then, he licked, slurped, and sucked. I grabbed his locks as he slid his fingers in and out of both holes between my legs. My feet were planted on the roof of the car, over my head. He sucked and finger fucked me until I damn near farted. I came in his mouth, and he kept eating until I came again. He didn't stop until I started screaming and giggling at the same time.

"Jacyn, baby, stop! Oh, my God!" I cried and laughed.

Jacyn smacked my ass, finally coming up for air and letting my legs fall to his shoulders. He looked up at me, watching my chest heave in and out as I came down from that orgasm. "Finished round one. Round two is after we eat." Jacyn sat up.

I sat up, too, reaching for his face. I kissed him before wiping our juices from his lips, chin, and goatee. "We can't go in there smelling like pussy, Jacyn!"

"How did it feel?" Jacyn grinned a little, watching my body still shivering.

"I need to get on birth control, asap! *That's* how it felt! We're going to have to get some condoms or something!" I watched Jacyn's smile dim. I sighed. "I want to enjoy life for a few more years before I have a baby. A baby changes everything. Look what happened today with the news of a baby on the way! Can I be enough for you for now? Do we have to add to this new experience right now? Does it have to be this urgent?" I grabbed my thong. There weren't any panties in that dress box, so I would have to throw those on underneath that dress.

"Guess I'm just scared this is all a dream, that's all." Jacyn watched me reach for my dress. "Make sure you pee when we get in the church. And do a quick wash up down there. You're going to leak a little, babe. And thank you." He picked up his pants from the floor and slid them up his legs.

"For what, boo?" I asked.

"For staying in the battle." Jacyn spoke softly as he got into his pants.

"You gonna stick to your med schedule, right?" I asked, watching him nod.

"Yeah, I'll stick to it," he promised me.

CHAPTER 5
Melody

"You ready?" Jacyn asked as he eyed me coming out of the lady's bathroom into the church lobby.

I had to get myself together, scrubbing off some of that makeup from when the strippers made me over at the club. Red glitter eye shadow, blush, and red lipstick didn't go with my pretty pink dress. The choke chain actually matched my dress, so I kept it on, letting the chain dangle between my breasts.

I walked over to where Jacyn stood waiting for me by the water fountain, in the center of the massive church lobby. That church looked like heaven's palace. I heard rumors that a person had to make a certain income to even be a member. There was no such thing as come-as-you-are in that church. Women had to wear dresses or skirts, heels, and a fancy hat. There were no Afros. Just braids and relaxers. Men had to wear suits, ties, dress shoes, and had to come clean shaved, hair kept. I think they even had fuckin' assigned seats. You were seated based on the amount of money you contributed to the church each month.

The membership of the church choir was passed down by the family member who preceded them. Members who weren't chosen by family heritage were voted in on Election Day like they were fuckin' state officials or some shit. Everything that church represented, I was against, and Jacyn felt it the moment he locked fingers with mine.

"We won't stay long." Jacyn looked me over a little, chuckling at the fact that I was walking funny as we walked through the lobby. I knew I was walking like a virgin who just got fucked for the first time. "Part two of Operation Mario Coins is in effect tonight when we get back to that hotel. We need to get our money's worth before our flight tomorrow morning. I changed our flight. I can't wait until Friday. I moved up the reservation and moved up our flight. First class to Greece. We're gonna have a good time."

"Mmm-hmm." I wasn't really paying him any attention as I looked around at the fancy decor that lined the hallways of the church. There was nothing holy or humble about that church. I knew when I saw pictures of some of the Biggs family members lining the walls; that church was anything but holy.

"You don't have to become a member of the church to formally meet my parents." Jacyn yanked on my hand a little, moving my body closer to his as we walked the halls toward the church. "You had brief words with my parents the night I signed those divorce papers."

"The only thing your mother said to me was, 'have a seat.' And the only reason she even spoke to me then was because of Joel. The fact that he followed me around that entire day, freeing up Scarlett so they could plan your future, was the only reason I was even welcome at your parents' mansion. I don't belong here," I assured Jacyn.

"Yeah, I used to wonder if I belonged here, too," Jacyn admitted as we approached the door which led down another hallway toward the dining hall.

We heard chatter through the double doors before Jacyn reached for the handle to open it. The moment Jacyn held the door open for me to step inside, the chatter stopped, and all eyes were on us. I gulped as I stood there, looking at everyone as Jacyn shut the doors behind us.

Jacyn walked around me, grabbing my hand along the way to lead me toward the enormous round table where his family and church members were sitting. There had to be about twenty people in the room. The only ones I recognized were Lydia, Kelsius, Jacob, their older brother, Marcellus junior, and Breelyn. Breelyn's eyes lit up when she saw me, and she nudged the girl sitting beside her before she whispered something to her little friend.

"About time the newlyweds came up for air." Jacob scoffed, looking one of the church ladies over as she piled food on the plate in front of him. Jacob's voice echoed through the small microphone alongside his placemat. The table was so massive, and the room was so gigantic that there needed to be microphones at the table for everyone to be heard. "I'm sending you my detailing bill, Jacyn."

Jacyn grinned, holding my hand to lead me over to the table where two empty chairs awaited us. "Remember when you borrowed my car while yours was in the shop last year and said you were taking Pastor Terrance's daughter out for a 'test drive'? How did that ride go? Was it smooth? Did you tell shawty's boyfriend about that ride?"

A girl at the other end of the table gasped before looking down at her plate, ignoring glares from Miss Lydia and the other church women in attendance. I guessed she was Pastor Terrance's daughter.

"Damn," Kelsius yelled, swiping through his phone as Jacyn and I took our seats alongside him. "Why is Bonnie calling me? And Ashlie? And Reese? What these bitches want from a nigga?"

"Kelsius!" Lydia gasped. "We are in a church!"

"Amen." Kelsius put up praying hands before putting his phone back in his pocket as he silenced the ringtone. "My bad, Ms. Lydia, I should have said what do these Jezebels want from a nigga? Is that better, shit?"

Lydia huffed at the fact that a few of the younger guests were giggling. I assumed young members of the choir around our age.

Probably a few of the girls Kelsius had fucked on after choir practice.

"Yes, keep that sense of humor when me and your father start charging you $3500 in rent to stay on the family compound," Lydia snapped. Before Kelsius could come back with a reply, she turned her attention to me and Jacyn. "Speaking of having a sense of humor, you two wasted no time getting married seventy-two hours after Jacyn's divorce from Melody was finalized."

"Hey, Mama. How are you? I'm doing well. I found the office suite for my new practice. Thanks for asking." Jacyn shook his head, looking at the spread of food on the other side of the room. "So, we just help ourselves?"

"I'll fix you and your new wife a plate, baby." One of the heavy-set older women got up from her seat to go over to the buffet setup.

"Thank you, Sister Pearline. Put some of Sister Ella Mae's blueberry cobbler on that plate, too!" Jacyn laughed.

"Okay, baby!" Sister Pearline laughed, sashaying her way to the buffet, looking like Gloria on *Waiting to Exhale* when Marvin was watching her walk away after she offered to fix him those leftover collard greens and cornbread, some candied yams, a little potato salad, fried chicken, peach cobbler and a few slices of ham.

"Jacyn," Lydia huffed, slamming her fork down on the table. "Scarlett's results were mixed up at the doctor's office. She called me this morning, asking me if I knew any lawyers to represent her when she sues Atrium for ruining her life. She would never have wanted that divorce if they hadn't told her she was dying! She wasn't in her right mind!"

"I know all about not being in my 'right mind', Mama. And I stayed and stuck it out, even when I couldn't remember my own name. I'm not trying to hear this. I'm trying to eat," Jacyn let his mama know.

There was silence for a few moments as we watched sisters of the church serve everyone seated at the table. The only noise in the room was silverware clinking together as everyone dug in.

"Forty-five days since you met this woman at the club." Lydia just kept pressing what she felt was an issue. "You spent less than a week with her. The only thing you know about her is that she can sing. No, there is another thing. She got into a fight with your ex-wife's best friend over your brother sitting over there."

Jacob smirked.

Kelsius sat up in his seat next to Jacyn. "Don't bring me in this shit. I just came here to eat with y'all. Dat's it."

Jacyn was trying to hold it together. His jaws started to twitch. The hydroxyzine was finally starting to calm him down, and they were trying to hype him back up. The nigga just killed a man, and we were sitting in a church like the shit never happened.

"Mama," Jacyn cleared his throat. "I prayed for a woman like Melody. I made a promise to God that if he made her my wife, I'd be the best husband for her. You really think I'm the type to let a woman dump me and pick me back up when she chooses? That's how weak you think I am?"

"No, what I think is you two are young and will make plenty of mistakes. Scarlett is sorry. And Scarlett is pregnant," Lydia revealed.

The guests whispered among each other before looking at Jacyn and me for a response.

"I'm aware." Jacyn watched Sister Pearline walk back over to us with two plates piled full of food.

"You're aware?" Lydia scoffed. "She's having your baby! She's already got one special needs son that she can barely handle! Don't you think she needs your help? Those kids need a two-parent household!"

"She's the one who left *me*, remember?" Jacyn watched Sister Pearline set my plate in front of me. The moment the plate landed in front of me, Jacyn grabbed his fork, digging into my mac-n-cheese before sticking the fork into some cinnamony candied yams. He put it to my lips, grinning as I opened my mouth to take a bite. "Good, huh? These sisters can cook. I've been eating like this since I was five, baby girl."

I glanced over at his mother, who didn't like the way that man was loving on me one bit.

Lydia rolled her eyes, looking totally disgusted by the man continuing to feed me from his favorite things on my plate. "Oh, I get it. So, Melody is a rebound?"

That shit had Breelyn gasping. "Oh, no," she muttered.

Lydia rolled her eyes from Jacyn over to Breelyn before looking back at Jacyn. "You're just using her to heal the pain? She's just a Band-Aid. She's—"

"Sitting right here." I laughed off his mother's stupidity.

"You quit your job at private school. What were you making, like $45,000 a year?" Lydia scoffed. "They call you The Virgin Melody at the club where your grandma and now your mother sells women and breaks up marriages. You bring no value to my son whatsoever. You can sing. I've seen your videos on social media; I'll give you that much. You couldn't sing in our choir without being voted in. And who would vote a woman into our choir who comes from a family of pimps and whores?"

"All this coming from the First Lady of a church who has members of the Biggs family on her walls? I'm pretty sure most of those men out there are the same men who pay for those prostitutes you say my grandmother and mother sell. As a matter of fact, my mama was one of the women sold to those men!" I told the bitch. "You don't wanna get me started! Jacyn, you better get her!"

Jacyn grabbed my hand. I think he was trying to calm himself more than he was trying to calm me. It seemed to upset him that I was upset. He took a deep breath before addressing his mama. "A rebound," he said after taking his breath, "is a person who fills a void left by your partner. A rebound is temporary relief. I can admit that Scarlett broke my heart when she ended things abruptly, with no remorse, but she fixed my vision. She made me see that it was never supposed to be her. Scarlett was the woman I could live with, but Melody is the woman I can't live without. She's far from a rebound. She's not my second choice. She's my *only* choice. If she was a rebound, don't you think I would've taken Scarlett back when she showed up at the hotel room with a folder full of proof? She's going to have to live with my choice, just like she made me live with hers."

Lydia laughed out loud. "See! This is revenge! You just don't want to be alone, Jacyn!"

Jacyn let go of my hand to scratch his head anxiously. "I was alone with that woman since we started dating, mama. I only married her because you made that decision for us when we were teenagers. Melody is *my* decision. You brought us here for *this*? Me and my *choice* could've been packing for Greece. Don't piss me off, Mama."

"I'm only saying," there Lydia was, trying to act like he was the one attacking her, when she was the one who started the fuckin' debate, "that you've spent ninety-five percent of your life with that women you're just dismissing for a woman you don't even know!"

"Yeah," Jacob spoke up, "and I'm watching your son while you're flying halfway around the world with this replacement."

Kelsius stayed out of the discussion until Jacob thought he was going to put his two cents in. "If I recall, his ex-bitch is the one who *chose* this 'replacement'. Whoever he replaced with that bitch doesn't have shit to do with you."

"You *would* take up for this replacement, seeing as though you *did* want her first, huh?" Jacob smirked.

Kelsius laughed mockingly. "A'ight, nigga, better chill before I replace your lungs with a ventilator. I'm just telling your stupid ass that I can watch my little nephew if bro needs me to. Last time Joel was with you, one of your hoes had my nephew eating fuckin' glue sticks."

"Watch your mouth, Kelsius." Marcellus tried to calm his younger brother.

"I ain't gotta watch shit," Kelsius snarled, about to dig into his food when his iPhone started ringing.

"Looks like one of your hoes is calling now," Jacob muttered.

"Exactly how many women *do* you have?" Lydia hissed.

"Hoes, Mama. How many *hoes* do I have," Kelsius corrected her. "It's the holiday season. Tis the season to be dashing through these hoes."

Lydia flipped her thick salt and pepper hair over her shoulder. "Why don't you dash through a few job applications while you're at it?"

Jacyn had had enough. "Not too much on my little brother, Mama. Kellz is going to be the office manager at my practice. He has a job."

"And exactly how long will he keep it, though?" Jacob commented.

"The same amount of time it takes me to reload this clip after I unload it on your muthafuckin' ass." Kelsius took his gun from his pants and set it on the table, turning in his seat toward Jacob.

"Aye, do you have to pull out your gun every time you come in this church?" Marcellus huffed.

"We just finished choir rehearsal! Jesus!" one of the women at the other end butted in. "All this arguing when I thought we were coming together to congratulate Jacyn and his new wife, not ruin their wedding night! And we haven't even said grace! Can we just pray and eat?"

Kelsius grabbed his gun from the table, putting it back in his pocket. "You're right, Sister Cierra." He closed his eyes and proceeded to pray. Well, his version of a prayer. "Lord, please don't send anymore stupid ass bitches to my life. Amen." He opened his eyes and started eating.

"Just ignorant. Lydia, your children are so disrespectful," one of the sisters commented, grabbing her food before getting up from the table and heading out of the ballroom.

Lydia frowned with embarrassment, then she looked over at Breelyn, who'd started eating her food. "So, Breelyn, how long are you in town?"

I thought she was fuckin' with my sister to fuck with me, but then I saw the look on Kelsius's face as he leaned back in his seat. "This bitch" was written all over his face.

And Jacob smirked.

Breelyn looked around at everyone who was looking at her while they ate their food. She sat up in her seat, clearing her throat. "Well, as you know, my mother's choir is in town this week for the gospel convention in Raleigh. I will be singing with your choir this weekend. And I bought a house here, so I'll be here permanently." She glanced at the irritated expression on my face before she looked back at Lydia. "These greens are so good." She laughed nervously.

Lydia wasn't letting up. "Oh, really? How does your father feel about you moving to own?"

Breelyn's nervous smile faded. "He's busy running that casino. He won't have time to worry about me. Probably won't even notice that I'm here."

Jacyn frowned as if he was trying to make sense of what she was saying. He thought for a moment before looking over at Breelyn. "Casino? Donovan Biggs is your father?"

Breelyn nodded. "Yup."

Lydia looked over at me. "Have you met your sister? You two must be around the same age. I'm sure you have lots in common." Lydia grinned devilishly.

Jacob butted in again. "Aye, didn't y'all two used to go together, Kelsius? Like in the eighth grade?"

Kelsius was getting sick of that nigga. "Aye, didn't you used to get your ass beat in the eighth grade, muthafucka?"

Jacob dug into his food, continuing to laugh. "Nah, for real. Why did y'all break up again? Because she wouldn't come up off that pussy? Because she wasn't like those fast-ass girls you used to run through?"

Kelsius leaned back in his chair, tossing the food around on his plate. "Nigga, I will unload every bullet in this gun off in your face if you don't stop fuckin' with me."

It all started to make sense as to why Kelsius hated virgins.

The fool had tried to fuck my sister, and she wouldn't give it up. Then, he ran into me some seven years later, and I wasn't giving it up either. And we just happened to be fuckin' sisters.

Jacyn turned to his brother, grabbing Kelsius's arm as he reached into his pants again for the gun that he was definitely ready to use. "Bro, go cool off."

Kelsius snatched away from Jacyn. "Nah, these bullets are about to cool off inside that nigga if he doesn't stop running his fuckin' mouth!"

"Lydia, your sons have no self-control," another sister with a blonde fade commented.

Kelsius laughed, getting up from his seat. "I know this bald-headed demon isn't talking shit when all her daughters are fuckin' the drummer. The nigga told me how he be beating their drums every night after choir practice. I'm sure he has a pussy appointment with one of them tonight. Shit, maybe all three of 'em!"

"Kellz, go outside and cool off!" Jacyn tried not to laugh at his brother.

"Man, one of y'all old ass ladies wrap my plate up. Jacyn, nigga, I'll be outside. I'm not riding with that nigga. I'll get one of y'all daughters to take me home." He winked at the pretty girl sitting next to Breelyn.

Breelyn frowned at Kelsius as he made his way out of the room, sparking a cigarette on his way out.

Jacyn laughed, digging into his food. "Swear little bro is crazy."

Lydia huffed. "Jacyn, this isn't funny."

"Mama, you're not gonna sit there and act like you didn't get him started. It was only a matter of time before he got tired of the way you were coming at me. You know how he is."

"That boy needs to be the first client at your new practice, not an employee!" Lydia exclaimed.

Jacyn looked at his mother like she'd lost it. "That *boy* is your son."

"*Adopted* son," Jacob butt in again.

Jacyn turned in his seat towards the idiot. "And you wonder why bro pulls out his gun every time you open your mouth. Y'all gotta give him some grace."

"Nah, what he needs are some of those pills you take." Jacob smirked before digging into his food.

I grabbed Jacyn's hand before he reached into his pants. We had enough shooting for one night. We didn't stay long after that. Maybe a good ten or fifteen minutes before we wrapped up what we couldn't eat. Breelyn and I exchanged glances a few times. I was sure she had just as many questions for me as I had for her.

"Bro, Marcellus said you could use his whip to drop me and 'the replacement' off at the hotel." Jacyn nudged me as we walked out the church doors.

Kelsius stood outside, smoking a cigarette. He frowned, watching us head down the steps and over to him. He took the plate Jacyn handed him before flicking his cigarette to the ground and stepping on it to put out the fire.

Jacyn shook his head at Kelsius's lack of a response before he tuned to me and kissed me on the forehead. "I'll pull the car around, baby."

"Okay," I whispered, looking up at him as he kissed my lips before he headed down the sidewalk.

"Y'all niggas make me sick with all that lovey-dovey shit." Kelsius clicked his teeth before grinning. "Nah, for real, I'm happy for my brother. He's happy with you. He needs that shit. I don't give a fuck what this fake-ass religious family says, he was *not* happy with that bitch. Ya know, Lydia would make comments about wanting light-skinned grandbabies with light eyes and shit. That's why she pushed them together. She wanted Joel to come out white. Let this baby come out white and watch her parade that baby around like it's a trophy. Sick ass bitch. I hate a colorist. We've been calling Scarlett 'white girl' so long that the bitch actually thinks she's white, and Lydia treats the bitch like she's white. The fuck be wrong with bitches? You wanna white baby, too? Because we're niggas. We create black, chocolate-ass babies. Have you seen my daughter that I blessed Bonnie with? My baby looks like a chocolate donut!"

"Oh, my goodness!" I burst out laughing. "I haven't seen her, but I bet she's a cutie with a description like that."

Kelsius nodded in agreement. "Her mama is a crazy bitch, but we created a beautiful baby. Swear I hate I fucked that red bitch. I hate myself every time I fuck her. I'll stop fuckin' her one day when my dick catches up with my brain."

"Typical." I rolled my eyes. "That bitch is crazy. Need to leave her alone before you get caught up. The girls at the club say she came into the club a few weeks ago, trying to shoot you *and* whatever bitch you showed up to the club with!"

"Baby, she's not the first bitch to try to kill a nigga. I've had this good, big, black dick for twenty-one years. I was supposed to be dead five bitches ago. I am not scared of that retarded muthafucka." Kelsius looked at me like I had him fucked up.

I rubbed my head, already too overstimulated to reason with him. He was not about to give me a fuckin' headache. So, I changed the subject. "So, you know my sister?"

Kelsius's eyebrows lowered, and he clicked his teeth, lying like a muthafucka. "Nah."

I hesitated before asking. "What's she like?"

Kelsius shrugged. "Used to be the sweetest girl when we were younger. Who knows what the world has done to her since I last saw her. Not too much, I hope. But that's a memory I'd rather leave where it is. Like I said, I don't know your sister, at least not anymore."

We both were silent for a few seconds before he thought about the fact that I referred to her as my sister.

"Did you know before tonight that she was your sister?" he hesitated to ask.

I shook my head. "I met her at the club tonight. Neither of us knew the other existed before today. It's been one hell of a day. I just want to go to sleep and try again tomorrow."

Kelsius agreed. "Yeah. We've seen enough for one day. At least you know you're in the hands of a muthafucka who doesn't play about you. Jacyn is fucked up about you, sis. He won't play about you, and I won't play about my brother. So, you good, a'ight?"

I nodded. "A'ight."

Kelsius shook off that sentimental shit that he was feeling. I knew because I felt the tears start to bubble up in my eyes, too. Kelsius wiped his eyes. "Fuck all that. Look, hear me out. Make sure he pops those pills at 8:00 a.m. and 5:00 p.m. every fuckin night, aight? I'll have one of my sugar mamas check on Jaliyah. And one of my nurse hoes will tell me how Belle is doing. Just... keep my brother calm. And y'all pop a few of these tonight." He dug into his pocket to pull out a Ziplock back of what looked like brown Haribo gummy bears.

"What are these?" I questioned as he handed the bag to me.

Kelsius smiled. "Edibles infused with a little Henny. We call them 'Hennything Is Possible.'"

"Oh, lord." I was nervous at the sound of that.

And Kelsius could see it all over my face. "Haha, enjoy, sis. And don't be stingy with the pussy. Big bro needs that shit tonight. Been talking about it for forty-five fuckin days. Shut his ass the fuck up, ya feel me?

Jacyn pulled up.

And we got inside

***

I don't know why I took that bag from Kelsius. And I don't know why I told Jacyn that his brother gave that shit to us. The moment we dropped Kelsius back off at his place, I showed Jacyn the bag he was digging in. He ate three. I ate just one. Everything was fine at first.

Twenty minutes later...

Don't ask me how the fuck we made it to our room because I really don't remember. As far as I remembered, we flew to that muthafucka on a unicorn's back. My students at the private school watched *My Little Pony* every day before nap time. Those ponies followed us to our room that night. I swear I was so high that I watched them dancing in a circle, singing Gunna's "WGFT". I do remember Jacyn looking totally unfazed by the gummies. He was taking my clothes off the moment we got inside. I don't know how the fuck we ended up on that balcony. Don't ask me how I ended up bent over the railing. Or how I ended up straddling his lap in that hot tub. Or how I ended up sitting on the toilet, suckin' his dick while I was peeing. Or warming KY Jelly in the microwave. Or lying on the bed, hanging over the edge while he fucked my face and dug in my pussy with something that vibrated and pulsated in and out of me. Or how we ended up fucking in our plane seats the next morning.

Salt water is what I smelled when I finally felt like myself again. Well, the hungover version of myself. The loud sound of planes crashing is what woke me up. Not to mention I was hot as fuck. I peeled myself from the softest sheets I'd ever felt and pushed my hair from my face, looking to my right to see Jacyn lying on his back, drooling, mouth wide open. I looked over on the nightstand alongside him. That pink chain lay next to all sorts of vibrators, butt plugs, whips, and chains. The fuck kind of time did we have that night?

When I tried to get up from the bed, oh, I felt the time we had for sure. My lips—the ones on my face *and* the ones between my legs—were sore. Not to mention my neck, my back, and my asshole. I felt like a power drill had fucked every hole on my body. I looked down at my pillow. Half of my damn individual lashes were on that muthafucka. The nigga done fucked my lashes off. What day was it?

I sat at the edge of the bed, looking around until my eyes landed on the ocean view right outside our window. I cringed and squealed silently as I got up from the bed, wobbling my ass over to check out the view. It was so beautiful, but the heat in the room had me dizzy the moment I got to the glass doors. I stumbled through the villa, looking for the thermostat. Once I found it, I gasped at the fact that the shit was on fuckin' ninety degrees. I turned the thermostat off, fanning myself as I walked away. But the moment I walked away, I heard beeping. I turned back around and walked back to the thermostat, eying the muthafucka click back on and turn up five more degrees.

"I must be still high. Yeah, that's gotta be it," I told myself before calling out for my husband. "Uhh, baby? Jacyn!"

After a few seconds, I heard footsteps and yawning.

"Mamas? You good? Why the fuck is it so hot in here?" Jacyn's voice approached.

I stared at the thermostat as I pressed the power button to turn the shit off. And it came right back on again. "Do you see this, or am I still high?"

Jacyn approached my side, rubbing his eyes before he reached for the power button himself to turn it off. And just as it did with me, it came right back on. Jacyn frowned. "The shit has been doing this all week."

I gasped loudly. "What? We've been here a week?" I turned around, facing the enormous villa, looking at the luxurious amenities that I'd been too high to fuckin' remember. And I started crying. "Jacyn! How many of those edibles did we have?"

"Baby, the whole bag." Jacyn laughed. "Three a day since last Tuesday, baby doll. We're just coming back down. We had a time every fuckin' night, baby." He gave me a hard smack on the ass before walking back through the house. "But yeah, hotel maintenance has been over every day to reset that shit. I don't know what's been up with it. Let's shower and go get some lunch at our favorite spot."

I burst out crying again. "*What* favorite spot?"

I'd never eaten so good in my life. The spread at Taverna Bar Vasilis was amazing. Goat, lamb, lobster, fish, steak, breads, dips, fruit, vegetables, wine, and lemonade. Jacyn dug into some of everything while I sat there in awe, staring out at the ocean. In Crete fuckin' Greece. I'd never been off the East Coast, let alone around the world. And I was sitting there with him. He acted like everything was completely normal, and I was just in awe. Life as I knew it was definitely changing before my eyes.

"Baby, you're not eating," Jacyn noticed, looking down at the plate of food in front of me that I hadn't even touched.

"My ass hurts." I told him, and he chuckled.

"I dug in it a little the last few days. You kept asking me to. You don't remember?" Jacyn asked.

And memories of me telling him to put his tongue in my ass flashed through my mind. "No," I lied, digging into my food.

"You're not a virgin anymore, Mrs. Oxberry." Jacyn smirked.

I rubbed my neck, which when I looked in the mirror to get dressed that morning, I noticed a red ring around it. "You choked the shit out of me, Jacyn."

Jacyn ran his fingers around this neck to show me the ring around his neck as well. "And you did the same to me."

My eyes widened a little as I looked back down into my food. "What the fuck did we do to each other?"

"Let out some frustrations." Jacyn scoffed.

"We look like fuckin' Ike and Tina after they whupped each other's ass in the back of that limo!" I exclaimed.

Jacyn nodded. "And we're gonna do that shit again tonight. The first night of our honeymoon, you told me to fuck you in ways that my ex-wife wouldn't let me. And from the moments I can remember, that's exactly what I did, at *your* request."

"I'm going to kill your fuckin' brother." I watched him laughing.

Jacyn looked over my shoulder. His laughter subsided as he caught sight of something it looked as if he didn't want to see. It looked like he was reaching for his gun, which he knew he couldn't bring to Greece for self-defense purposes. He didn't think he would need it.

When I looked over my shoulder, I saw just why he reached for that muthafucka. There Scarlett was, strolling through the shaded area outside the restaurant like she was fuckin' Marilyn Monroe.

"How did you two like the heat in your villa? Do you know there's an app to control the thermostat in your room? Technology is a beast. Welcome to hell, bitch!" Scarlett barely made it halfway down the center of the outdoor dining area when I heard Kelsius's voice calling out to her.

"Aye, hoe. The fuck you think you're doing?" Kelsius got Scarlett's attention. He had two Greek women with him who looked like they boxed for a living.

My eyes widened as I looked back at Jacyn, folding my arms.

He said back calmly in his chair, continuing to eat his food. "Oh, yeah, Kelsius flew in last night. Said he heard Scarlett found out where we were headed and was on her way here. You gonna eat your steak?"

"Your wedding vows said, 'no weapon against us will prosper.' Remember that shit, Jacyn?" I huffed.

Jacyn nodded. "Yeah, I did. I never said the weapon wouldn't form, though. I just said it wouldn't *prosper*. Is she prospering, mamas? Now eat."

I was about to respond to him when my phone rang. My heart leaped at the sight of Belle's name on my caller ID. I tuned out Scarlett arguing with Kelsius as I answered her call. "Belle!" I shrieked.

"How's the mediterranean, bitch?" Belle laughed through the phone.

I looked over my shoulder, watching the two gladiator chicks escort Scarlett out away from the restaurant. "Girl," I shook my head, "you wouldn't believe me if I told you."

CHAPTER 6
Belinda "Belle" Maybach

"Nigga, what? Scarlett's bitch ass is out there?" I sat up in my hospital bed, listening to Mellie tell me about the fact that Scarlett showed up to their honeymoon halfway around the fuckin' globe. Who the fuck was feeding Scarlett the information? Had to be someone close to the family to know Jacyn's exact location.

"This bitch was controlling the heat in our room with a fuckin' app on her phone!" Mellie squealed. "Kelsius's hoes just snatched her up and got her the fuck away from this restaurant. Can't even enjoy the beach while I eat my steak, cheese eggs, and potatoes."

"The bitch just mad 'cause Chante's got a man at home." I snickered a little, sitting up in the hospital bed, the IV line tugging at my hand. I grimaced, rubbing my hand. "And Kelsius is out there? The fuck? This a family trip or some shit, and I'm in this damn hospital?"

"I think that boy is scared to leave his brother's side. When you see one, you see the other," Mellie whispered. "I gotta go, Ballerina." She called me by my occupation. "I'm here until tomorrow. Been high the entire time I've been here and don't remember a fuckin' thing!"

I laughed out loud, eying a nurse coming into my room after a quick tap on the door. "Sounds like you two been choppin'-n-screwin'! My baby is a woman now! I can't wait to hear how he flipped your cervix every way but loose!"

Mellie screamed out with laughter. "I cannot with you! Love you to the moon…"

"And beyond." I blew her a kiss before hanging up the phone, exhaling sharply.

The nurse wasn't there to help me. She was my mother's nurse from ICU, and she was keeping me updated on my mother's progress. I didn't have to ask how my mother was doing because her solemn expression said everything I needed to know.

"Your stepfather is pulling the plug on Miss Ethel in one—" Nurse Lucille barely got the words out of her mouth before I pushed back my sheets and was about to pull my fuckin' IVs out myself.

Nurse Lucille rushed over to me to stop me from rushing to save a woman who was already gone.

I tried to shove the nurse away, but she grabbed me by my forearms, pulling my body into hers for a tight hug. My mama had been fighting for her life over the past year. My stepfather's gambling addiction almost lost them their butcher shop. Mama worked long hours to get them out of the debt her husband put them in, while I worked long hours to pay the bills in not just their household, but mine. All the stress of picking my drunk stepfather up from a bar or a casino took a toll on my mama, because while she was taking care of him, no one was taking care of her.

I met Tevin when I was ten years old. Mama had inherited the Maybach Butchers, my grandfather's corner store and butcher shop. He had the hook on the best meat in town. Beef, pork, chicken, steak, deer, goat, fish. You name it, Maybach had it. My biological father was killed in battle while deployed to Afghanistan. I don't have many memories of him outside of mama dragging me with her to whichever bitch's house he was laid up at. If he wasn't deployed, he was working late nights, every night. My mama caught that man with at least three women a week, that much I do remember. So, when she met Tevin, I was happy for her. She had a man who came home to her every night. He got up at 7:00 to go to work as a security guard at the prison and came home every night at 7:00, where Mama had a plate of hot food waiting for him. We were one big, happy family until...

Tevin's brother came up missing. His brother was Randy Carter, Mellie's grandmother's husband. No one had seen the man. Miss Latisha (Mellie's grandmother) put out a police report when he didn't show up at her house for a few days. Tevin was losing his mind over his little brother, the only sibling he had left after his other brother had been killed by his wife when she caught him cheating. Tevin had gone out drinking with his boys and had come back late night. Mama wasn't home. She'd gone out with Miss Latisha like they did every Saturday night. They'd play poker down at the Midnight Ballet in one of the VIP rooms. Tevin came home yelling, drunk as fuck, looking for my mama. He went digging in her drawers, trying to figure out what outfit she was wearing when he came across a watch owned by Randy. A watch that their father had given to Randy was a birthday gift when he was in high school.

Tevin assumed my mama was fuckin' his brother and knew where he was. I didn't want him mad at my mother, so I told him that I was the one who had found the watch, and I found it in his car one day when Mama was driving me home from school. He was so drunk that he bought that story. He had me warm up whatever leftover food mama had for him in the fridge. She didn't make him anything, too busy running the meat market that day. I was up at 12:35 a.m. frying that man two chicken thighs, rice, gravy, and baked beans. He was telling me stories about his childhood while drinking three or four more bottles of beer.

I started to feel uncomfortable when he began telling me about his first sexual experience. When I attempted to excuse myself to go to my room, the nigga grabbed me by my wrist, asking me if I'd ever been with any of those poor little niggas at my school, who were never gonna be shit but drug dealers and inmates. I told him that I was only fuckin' twelve, and I was still playing with fuckin' Barbies and Brat Dolls. And that's when he pulled me onto his lap and said he was going to check and see if I was lying. That he could tell if I was a virgin or not.

There I was, in a tug of war with a man in his late forties. I'd never been what you call skinny. I'd always had thighs and ass, even in middle school. Boys in middle school would tease me, whereas boys in high school or college would fuck with me whenever I went out with my friends. I couldn't go to the skating rink without some junior or senior trying to feel me up. And I'd get invitations to college parties. Everyone knew I was twelve. Shit, everyone knew me because my mama's best friend owned a fuckin' strip club where either their daddies went every night or their mamas danced/sold pussy.

What started off as a struggle ended with me having my first orgasm on that pervert's lap. He let me off his lap, smacked my ass and told me to go to sleep before my mama got home. And the next night, he did the shit again, only it wasn't his fingers that time, it was his dick. And I liked that shit, too. I was a kid. I knew the shit was wrong, but I was confused by why my body reacted to him the way it did. Every night for six weeks, that nigga was in my bedroom while Mama was late night helping Ms. Latisha at the club.

The night police found Randy's car in the Catawba River was the last night I had sex with Tevin. I was running a fever and started cramping. Mama took me to the hospital, only to find out that I was pregnant. Tevin never touched me again, probably thinking his brother's missing person's report turning into a possible murder was his karma for touching someone he had no business touching.

"Belinda, you're about to be discharged. Let me take your IVs out. Discharge takes a while, so if you want, you can go over and say your goodbyes to your mother before they pull the plug. Do you need a wheelchair?" Nurse Lucille asked me.

I shook my head. I had been treated like a fuckin' drug addict that entire week. Yeah, I popped some pills and snorted some shit that night Dawnna had me booked to perform at local rapper Da Entity's mansion in Ballantyne. The last time I was booked for one of his events, I felt like I was at fuckin' Junior's bachelor party. I'd barely finished fuckin' one nigga when the next nigga was walking in the door. They'd locked me in a room for five hours, did what they were permitted to do to me by Dawnna. I had to be high to endure the shit they'd do to me.

Once my stomach was pumped, and I was put on IV fluids, it still took a few days for the drugs to come out of my system. And once the drugs wore off, I started hallucinating. Tried to injure nurses and stab a few med techs with my IV needles. I was moved to the fifth floor and put on antipsychotic meds. A psychiatrist came and talked to me, blah, blah, blah. Once they realized my episodes were in response to the drugs I was on and not a chemical imbalance, they agreed that I could go home in a few days. That Tuesday marked my eighth day at the hospital.

Nurse Lucille (one of the nurses that I ended up hitting over the head with a dinner tray when I ran down the halls, trying to escape the aliens that were in my room during my second night in the hospital) helped me slip into a second hospital gown that she put on backward to act as a bathrobe over my other hospital gown. She got transport to come take me to say my last goodbyes to my mother.

But when I got to her room, nurses were already apologizing to Tevin for his loss. And I fuckin' lost it. I jumped out of the chair and few over the nigga who never acknowledged the damage he caused. The damage I never told anyone about. As a child, I thought it was better that I was the one abused instead of watching my mother get abused. I carried that weight inside me my entire life. Hypersexual is the term I've heard to describe my addiction to sex. And it wasn't so much of an addiction as it was taking back something that had been taken from me. It was more a compulsion than an addiction.

There I was, trying to strangle my stepfather. Nurses raced into the room, trying to pull me off him. So much for being discharged that day. Next thing I knew, I was waking up, cuffed to the railing of a hospital bed. I turned over to see Jacob Oxberry, Jacyn's younger adopted brother, sitting in the corner of my room, exhaling vapors from a gold THC pen.

"Ewww…" I huffed, watching that sexy chocolate nigga, with the most disrespectful mouth I've seen on any man, lean forward, resting his elbows on his legs.

That sexy asshole wore a suit everywhere he went. I didn't think he owned any regular clothes. He'd come to the club with his brothers every other night. He made the ballerinas (strippers at the Midnight Ballet) work for his hard-earned dollars. Damn near had to do Chris Brown backflips to get money from that muthafucka. Why the fuck was he in my room?

"'Ewwww' is how you've been treating the staff at this fuckin' hospital. You damn near scratched the nurse's eyes out the other day for pulling the plug on your mother." He shook his head at me, taking another hit from his pen.

My irritated expression faded as I looked over at the dry erase board on the wall. The date October 31. "I've been asleep four fuckin' days?" I looked over at him. "I've been cuffed to this bed for four days?"

Jacob shook his head. "Nah. You woke up a few times, screaming and asking for your mother. They had to sedate you about three times. I told them I had a nurse on duty on the compound who could look out for your mental wellbeing. She's one of the nurses that's going to be at bro's practice once he opens in November. Nurses who will help administer meds to his patients who need more than music therapy to suppress those suicidal tendencies."

I sat up in my bed. "Nigga, I'm not suicidal."

Jacob nodded toward both of my bandaged wrists. "You dug

into your wrists with a screw you took out of the bed the other night. Explain that."

My heart pounded in my chest. "Where's Melody? Is she back from her honeymoon?"

"It's been storming the last few days. Their flight got delayed. Jacyn decided to stay in Greece another week with The Replacement." Jacob sounded irritated at the thought of Melody and Jacyn together, so much so that he had to give her a stupid ass nickname.

"That *replacement* is the best thing to ever happen to your brother, Jacob. Now that he isn't tied to that white woman your family loves so much, he can focus on his own success. Doesn't he write music? Shit, don't *you* write music? You're just mad because Jacyn can live his life to the fullest while you're stuck producing and writing music for your family for room and board. I'm sure your older brother, Marcellus, is going to inherit that gospel recording company when your parents take a dirt nap. Calling Melody 'The Replacement' is crazy." I smacked my teeth. "I read this book by Prince Harry called 'The Spare'. That's you, nigga. *You* are the spare."

Jacob sat back in his seat, his dark eyes glaring a little before he chuckled. "I'm surprised you read. Most prostitutes are too busy fuckin' and suckin' to read a book. I heard you missed a great party that night. One of my producer homies was at The Entity's party. Said he paid Dawnna $50,000 to let him piss on, shit on, and choke those strippers. Those strippers might have taken home $2000 that night, when Dawnna racked in about $80,000 to send in five ballerinas. And here you are, acting crazy about your stepfather pulling the plug on a woman who would let her daughter degrade herself every night. Your mama was best friends with Ms. Latisha! Your mama let her best friend pimp you out, then let her best friend's daughter do the same shit to you. And you're *crying* over this bitch?"

I didn't even realize I was crying until I felt the tears slide across the bridge of my nose as I reached over to try to yank my wrist loose from the bed. "I don't even know why you're here. I'm not going anywhere with you, Jacob."

There was a tapping at the door before it opened, and the doctor peeped her head inside. I vaguely remembered her. I think I may have smacked her for thinking she was trying to strangle me with her stethoscope.

The blonde-haired, middle-aged woman smiled with her blue eyes before greeting me. "Well, Ms. Maybach, you're not going to smack me when I check your heart rate, are you?" she joked.

I pursed my lips. Yeah, that was her. I eyed her badge as she sat down on a metal stool and scooted over to my bedside. "I might, Doctor Stewert. I just might."

Her smile faded a little, pausing before she attempted to remove her stethoscope from around her neck. "I'll just check your previous vitals from when the nurse took them a few hours ago. We had to tie at least one wrist to the bed for safety reasons. You're not under arrest. No one is pressing charges. However, I'm referring you to a therapist. Mr. Oxberry here says that he highly recommends his brother, Jacyn Oxberry, who can see you right away when he returns from his honeymoon. In the meantime, we can't let you go home unless we can ensure your safety. We just want to make sure you weren't adversely affected by the meds we put in your system when you overdosed. We gave you naloxone, which is used to reverse an overdose. Hallucinations are rare, but they can happen on this type of drug because they cause immediate withdrawal symptoms in drug addicts."

I shook my head frantically. "I'm not a fuckin' addict!"

Doctor Stewert removed her glasses. "The amount of drugs in your system could've killed everyone on my shift tonight. The only way I can release you is into the care of someone who will watch over you for the next two weeks. Mr. Oxberry has agreed to let you stay at his place under his nurse's care. The hospital is signing you over to her care at the registrar's desk."

I huffed, pushing the blankets off my legs with my free hand.

"I'm not staying with this muthafucka! I'm going home, to my apartment, on West Blvd, old lady."

"No, young lady," Doctor Stewart scoffed, "it's either you go home with Jacob, or every person you assaulted over the past two weeks will press charges on you, and you will be going home to a bunk in a jail cell downtown. A few of the nurses you assaulted are wives of the men that women like you call tricks. These women would love to send you to jail for not just assault, but prostitution. All you need to do is lay in bed for two weeks. Laying down on your back shouldn't be too hard for you, now should it, when you do that every night for employee?"

"Damn." Jacob smirked as the doctor got up from her stool.

My eyes widened at that unprofessional bitch. "Now I remember why I tried to choke you with that fuckin' stethoscope! Unprofessional ass bitch!"

"I know how much you like wearing those handcuffs, but the security will be in here as soon as your discharge papers are ready." The doctor winked at me before heading out of the room.

I folded my arms, sitting there watching Jacob laughing at me.

* * *

"Good lovin', body rockin', knockin' boots all night long, yeah. Makin' love until we tired, to the break of dawn." Jacob sang along to his dumb-ass '90s play list. The nigga sounded annoyingly soothing. Everything he did got on my nerves. He was doing all the right things, and I knew that nigga was some bullshit.

Jacob had just called some nurse he knew who worked at the Shady Pines Psychiatric Hospital where Mellie's sister, Jaliyah, had been transferred. Apparently, the nigga was part of the clinical team responsible for Jaliyah's well-being while she was briefly a resident at Devereaux Downes. He was a case manager for Devereaux Industries and could check on her progress. I had no idea he worked in the health care field. He was just as much a party animal as Kelsius. I saw those two bump heads many nights at the club, but let anyone outside of the family fuck with either of them, and it was off with that nigga's head.

After ensuring that Jaliyah was transitioning well into her stay at a new facility, the nigga had called to check on his mother who was worrying herself sick about Jacyn. Sounded like the family had a disagreement that night that I don't even remember being rushed to the hospital. Jacyn hadn't reached out to anyone but his brothers since he left the states. Jacob reassured his mother that Jacyn was fine and would return home when he was finished drilling a few new holes into his new wife.

Then, after that, the nigga called the sound engineer at his family's recording studio to make sure everything was set up for that weekend, so he could record the background vocals for one of his family's new singles. Then, after *that*, he called his mother back to let him know he was picking up Jacyn's son, Joel, to take his ass trick-or-treating that night. Ugh, he was making me sick. What was he about to do next? Stand on a corner on Sugar Creek and hand our syringes to the drug addicts who were sleeping at the bus stops?

"Nigga, please shut the fuck up," I muttered. "Heaven and the fuck that, all that shit."

"But, oh, come on, come on and turn the lights down. And let me get on it, yeah." He continued singing one of my mama's favorite H-Town songs.

"My mama used to fuck my stepfather on the table to this song. I do not wanna hear this shit." I reached for the volume, and Jacob pushed my hand away.

"Don't touch my shit," Jacob hissed.

"Look," I huffed. "I just wanna stop by my mom's place to get a few things. Then, I need to go to my place to pack a spinnanight bag. The doctor didn't say you needed to be up my fuckin' ass like a butt plug for two weeks."

"You think I'm about to drop you off, so you can go sell some tricks-n-treats tonight?" Jacob scoffed. "Nah, mamas, we're going to go pick up my nephew."

I made a face. "Why?"

"Because he's my fuckin' nephew, that's why," Jacob answered offensively. "We're taking him trick-or-treating. He dressed up as Spiderman last year. This year, me and him are going as the Smokestack Twins. I'ma be Stack. You can be Mary."

I rolled my eyes from staring out at the road to that nigga and watched him chuckle. "Oh, isn't that cute. A saint dressing up as a *Sinner*."

Jacob's smile faded. "I ain't no saint."

I nodded. "Oh, nigga, I know." I sank back in the passenger seat. "Do you have a cigarette? I need a damn cigarette. Or let me hit that pen you were using earlier."

Jacob shook his head. "Nah. You don't need anything in your system when the doctor clears you from Nurse Annie Jackson's care. The doctor meant what she said about pressing charges on you if you don't let someone take care of you while your body weans off the inhibitors and painkillers they had you on for the past two weeks. Now, I got you a fuckin' dress yesterday to wear when we go out trick-or-treating tonight."

"You don't even know what size I wear." I rolled my eyes, looking over at him as he glanced back at me.

"Your bra size is thirty-six DD. Your waist is twenty-seven. And your hips are thirty-six. You have a small waist and an ass that looks like two bitches getting in a fight when you walk. You have a hard time finding jeans that don't leave that huge gap around your waist. So, you usually only wear dresses, skirts, or jump suits. Your dress size is medium depending on the brand and the stretch. I bought you a champagne-colored, Serita silk maxi dress from Neiman Marcus."

I sat up in my chair, looking up at him as he gripped the steering wheel of that clean Maserati. "What? That dress is part of the LA'gence collection! That dress is $595!"

Jacob nodded. "Yeah. I know."

"You think I'm finna suck you up or something, bitch? 'Cause I'm the fuck not!" I told him.

Jacob shook his head, pulling that THC pen out of his pocket to take a few pulls. "Haven't you had enough sex for a lifetime? I don't want that soggy shit."

"Well, nigga, good, because I don't want that dity shit you got either!" I hissed, rolling my eyes and my neck. "You done been with every Midnight Ballerina in the club *but* me, nigga. It's gonna take more than $595 to get any of these tricks-in-treats I got."

"Just wear the fuckin' dress when we take my little nephew to get some candy. We won't be long. I'm only bringing you with me because you're not going back to that club. Bro told me to keep you away from there, so The Replacement doesn't go there looking for you. Two niggas got shot behind your friend hitting the stage that night to make that money you needed for your mama's hospital stay." Jacob told me something I didn't know.

"What?" I asked, wrapping the hoodie he'd given me earlier around myself tighter. "Mellie didn't mention that shit on the phone when I talked to her last week."

"Why would she? Wasn't like you told her that your mother was dying." Jacob sounded defensive, like he was the one I was withholding information from. "Dawnna turned the green light on while ole girl was on stage."

I knew Dawnna was evil, but I never thought she'd let the sharks loose on her daughter. The Sharks were the niggas who sat along the stage during our big performances. They'd wait for the greenlight to flash, so the first nigga who asked the security guard for the girl on stage could get first dibs for the night. That nigga had the option to pay for that girl for an hour. He could take her in one of the sugar rooms and get all the sugar he could handle for an hour. And trust me, those niggas would get their money's worth.

"I need to see that bitch tonight," I hissed.

Jacob looked at me like I'd lost my mind. "Nah, I just told you that you're not stepping a foot back in that club. Jacyn shot and killed the nigga who tried to drag Melody off stage. And Kelsius shot the nigga who was with that nigga! Bonnie and Scarlett were there when that shit went down. I'm sure they have motives for not saying shit, but it's only a matter of time, so stay the fuck out of that place, a'ight?"

"No," I responded. "No, I'm not going to the club. It's 6:00 on a Saturday. I know exactly where Dawnna is."

Every Saturday, Dawnna was fuckin' on Tayvon Best, the son of the health inspector, Nicholas Best. The little nigga was twenty-five and lived near UNC Charlotte. Dawnna fucked that nigga every Saturday while his parents took their mini vacation. Truth was, Dawnna was in love with Nicholas, but he was never leaving his wife of thirty years for a woman who ran a fuckin' whore house. So, Dawnna fucked on his son as her revenge.

Jacob was reluctant to pull up to that apartment building where Tayvon stayed, but he knew by the look on my face that I'd only end up eventually sneaking away from him to find Dawnna and kill her for her attempt at hurting my best friend. And on her fuckin' wedding night?

I looked back at Jacob, who had gotten out of his car and stood alongside it, keeping an eye on me. Tayvon's apartment was on the first floor of the apartment building and faced the street. I banged on the fuckin' door like I was the landlord, demanding my got-damn rent. I felt like Diamond when she showed up to the Playa's Club after Ronnie had Cousin Ebony do Junior's bachelor party. Had to fight off the urge to say, "Ebony got raped at Junior's bachelor party, and you left her there, didn't you?" Soon as Dawnna said she didn't know what I was talking about, I was gonna rock her shit.

The door flew open after the fourth bang. Lil Tayvon pulled the door open, ready to go the fuck off on me. "Man, who in the *fuck* is bangin' on my muthafuckin'—" His frown dissipated when he looked into my face and realized who I was. "BeeBee, the fuck are you doing here?" The nigga wiped his mouth, probably wiping Dawnna's pussy juice from his lips. He wasn't wearing a shirt, and his pants were unzipped. He'd just pulled out of the pussy to answer the door.

"Where's Dawnna Bill?" I asked, hands in my pockets.

He frowned in confusion, not recognizing the nickname I'd given my pimp. "Who?"

"Nigga, don't fuckin' play with me," I growled. "Where the fuck is she?"

"I'm here, Bag of Money." Dawnna laughed, approaching Tayvon from behind. She placed her hand on his shoulder, pulling him out of the way. "Excuse me while I pay my respects to her mama," she told the youngin'.

He looked me over before walking away.

"You look good for a drug addict." Dawnna looked me over as well, like she did every night before she sent me out to suck some dick. "If you came over to ask for the money to bury your mama, I don't have it. But if you're trying to make some money tonight, I have eight of your regulars ready with their dick in their hands right now. I'll even let you get thirty percent of the earnings, so your mama can have a nice little pine box." She smirked a little. "She can lay her bitch ass in a grave next to my mama. Though, if I were you, I'd cremate the bitch. The devil done gained two demons in the past three years."

My blood was boiling. I was trying to keep my thoughts together. She was a beautiful muthafucka, but they claim Satan was one of God's most beautiful creations, so that made sense. "Why the fuck did you turn the greenlight on Melody? Why would you do that shit, when I hear all she was trying to do was make the money back to take care of my mama's hospital bill!"

"See," Dawnna pointed her manicured figure at me, "that's both of your problems—always worried about one another. You need to worry about your muthafuckin' self. She wouldn't have been on that stage if you hadn't OD'ed, junkie bitch. I can see why you have to get high to function. I heard it was your steppappy who pulled the plug. I heard you have a special relationship with him."

My hands started to shake as I shook my head at her. "You're the one who needs to worry about *your* muthafuckin' self."

She went on to say some shit that was totally out of pocket. "Ya know, I never understood why your mother would let her best friend pimp her own daughter out. So, I asked her one day, and she told me the reason. Did you know that when you were twelve, your mama came home from the club early to see you bouncing up and down on Tevin's lap?"

I gasped. "Wh-what?"

Dawnna checked her nails before flipping her silky hair over her shoulder. "Yeah, your mama knew you were fuckin' her man. That's exactly why she helped my mother get rid of Tevin's brother's body that day he tried rape my daughter. And that's why she sent you to work at that club after you had that miscarriage."

My entire body shook as I gripped the gun in my pocket. The gun I'd gotten from under the passenger seat in Jacob's car.

"She couldn't believe her own daughter was fuckin' her man," Dawnna said in my face. "She said you looked like you were enjoying yourself. That you didn't look like a fuckin' victim."

"I was twelve. He was a fuckin' grown ass man!" I choked on my words as the memories started flashing back.

"Ethel said all she could think about was how your father used to cheat on her. When she saw you fuckin' her nigga, she saw your father fuckin' all those women he cheated on her with. And that since you wanted to fuck for free, you were gonna fuck and earn her some money. Still wanna give your mama a proper burial now?" Dawnna didn't get to finish her sentence before I pulled the gun out on her, cocking it back before putting it in her face.

That loud metal clinking got not just Tayvon's attention, who wasn't too far away from his cougar and knew I wasn't there to just talk, but caught Jacob's attention as well.

And Jacob was running down the sidewalk toward me when he realized I'd gotten a hold of his gun.

"Yo, yo, yo, chill!" Tayvon yelled at me.

Jacob was calm as ever as he approached me. He stood alongside me, eyeing Tayvon, who looked like he was ready to take a bullet for Dawnna. "Nigga, shut your bitch ass up," Jacob told the nigga before looking at his gun that I was aiming at Dawnna's face. "Belle, you just got out of the hospital."

"I was only twelve years old!" I screamed at the bitch, finger over the trigger.

Dawnna nodded. "So was I." She wasn't even trembling as she looked down the barrel of my gun.

"I didn't mean to do that shit! It felt good! I was confused!" I told her. "I knew I was wrong, but it felt good! And Mama knew? Mama blamed *me*?"

Dawnna nodded. "She did. Mamas always do." She even laughed a little. "Let that bitch burn in hell and move on with your life."

"You knew what I've been through, and you put me through some more shit?" I screamed.

"Shit, you like niggas raping you, remember?" Dawnna laughed right when the gun went off, bullet flying right over her ear and hitting the wall behind her.

The only reason I didn't shoot the bitch in her face was because my hand was shaking so bad that my aim was off.

"Got damn!" Tayvon screamed as Jacob grabbed the gun from me.

Dawnna's bright brown eyes glared into mine as Jacob took the gun from me. Just when she thought she was going to step through the doorway and lunge at me, Jacob put the gun to her forehead, mushing her head back, and pushing her back into the house.

"Baby, I won't miss, I promise you. She doesn't work at your club anymore. She doesn't exist in your fucked up world anymore. And if you come near her, *you* won't exist anymore. Whoever you send after her, I'll send right back after you. Whatever you pay them, I'll triple that shit. Just get back in that apartment and finish suckin the nigga off. He looks scared. He thought he lost you for a second." Jacob grabbed my trembling wrist.

But I wouldn't budge. I wanted more answers. I needed to know why she'd watch all those women who worked for her go through the same shit that she did. That *we* did. I hadn't enjoyed sex since I had that miscarriage. Since God punished me for what I'd done with my stepfather. Every encounter I had with sex was forced. I'd never enjoyed it, no matter how much money I made. I was numb. I hated who I was and had no idea that my mother hated me for who I was, too. She knew all along and pretended she didn't.

"Belle, let's go," Jacob told me, gun still in his hand, aiming it toward Dawnna and her scary ass boy toy. "Go to the fuckin' car."

I couldn't move my legs. My mind went blank as I immediately flashed back to having that D&C to remove some of the birth material that was left in me after my miscarriage. "I was twelve years old." I repeated it at least three times.

"You're not twelve anymore," Jacob said. His hand moved from my wrist to my hand, grabbing it in his and intertwining his fingers with mine. "That man at the hospital with your mother did this shit to you, not the other way around. You are not a victim; you survived."

"Barely." My voice shook.

Jacob glared at Dawnna. "Go inside and shut the fuckin' door. Say another fuckin' word, and I will shoot you in your mouth. You've said enough. You've done enough. You have five days to turn that club around before a nigga *burns* it down. I'm not talk. I'm action."

Tyvon pulled Dawnna away from the door and slammed it. He wasn't raised the way we were. The street life only existed in his damn AirPod Max's. We lived that shit every day. I was sure his first instinct was to call the cops, but I knew Dawnna had other plans.

CHAPTER 7
Belle

My vision became blurry, and I felt faint. PTSD is a bitch. It reveals itself at the most inconvenient times. I was supposed to shoot that bitch in her face. Instead, I was hyperventilating in Jacob's arms as he carried me to the car. I don't even remember how I ended up in his arms that night. And I definitely don't remember him putting me in the guest bed at his place until I woke up to the sound of glass clinking.

I turned over to see a nurse stirring honey into an oversized coffee mug. I frowned at the bitch, but she smiled down at me.

"Hi, I'm Rose." She smiled, her brown cheeks plumping. "I'll be your nurse here at the Oxberry Compound for your two-week stay."

I sat up, looking around at a bedroom that was bigger than my damn apartment. I looked up at the ceiling that seemed as high as the Sistine Chapel. Then, I looked at aqua blue and gold Elizabeth bedding by Michael Amini. I recognized that luxury bedding set because I added that $1,265.65 bedding set to my Wayfair cart that I never seemed to empty. My imagination had the same expensive taste as Jacob, apparently.

I quickly pushed the comforter off my legs to be even more

annoyed by the silk sheets underneath it. I didn't feel that a girl like me deserved any of that luxury. Jacob could've just let the doctor press charges on me. At least in jail I'd get a little vacation from everyone and everything on the outside for a little while. I'd just shit and piss on myself to keep anyone from turning me into their bitch.

"This is too much," I huffed, as the nurse handed me the mug of tea.

She agreed, looking around at the expensive décor, before looking back at me. "It is. But that's an Oxberry for you. Always going above and beyond for someone they care about. Mrs. Melody Oxberry told me to make sure I take good care of you while she's away. She told me to tell you, and excuse my language, 'Bitch, behave.'" She winked at me and walked for what seemed like a mile before reaching the door. "If you need anything, my number is on that card, which is on the nightstand."

I looked over at the card, then back at the door as she disappeared behind it. I sighed before taking a sip of the tea, which was actually pretty good, and I hated tea. As I took a few sips, I heard singing coming from behind the door.

"Somebody take meeeeee in your arms tonight!" Jacob came into the room, carrying Jacyn's son, Joel, in his arms.

I'd never seen anything more adorable in my life. Jacob was wearing a blue hat, blue vest, blue tie, crisp white shirt, blue dress pants, and Tramezza plain toe Oxford Ferragamos. And little Joel was dressed the same except that his hat, tie, and vest were red. And his cute little shoes were black velvet Chambelimoc Night Strass Christian Louboutin loafers. I didn't even know they made shoes that small. My heart was melting in my chest at the sight of those two dressed like the Smokestack Twins from *Sinners*. Joel was smiling from ear to ear with his jack-o'-lantern dangling from his tiny hands.

A Hispanic woman was behind them, smiling just as hard as Joel was and holding out her hands to take Joel from Jacob's arms. But he wouldn't budge.

"How does the song go, Joe-Joe?" Jacob smiled into the little boy's face.

And the little boy hummed like Preacher Boy. "Mmm-mmm-mmm-mmmmmm…"

Jacob laughed, and the maid or nanny or whoever she was laughed out loud, while I just burst out crying.

Jacob looked at me before looking back at Joel. "She's crying." He pointed over to me.

Joel looked at me before looking back at Jacob. "Crying?"

Jacob nodded. "I need to talk to her. Okay? So, go with Julianna, okay?"

Joel looked disappointed, but he nodded anyway, letting Julianna take him from Jacob's arms. Jacob watched the two of them leave the room before he closed the door behind them, removing his hat.

I quickly dried my face. "I'm sorry. It's been a long day. What time is it?"

Jacob looked at the watch on his wrist. "11:45. We went to all the mansions in the neighborhood. All the pretty, lonely wives gave us candy."

I rolled my eyes, the tears stopping instantly. "Nigga, I bet."

He chuckled a little, walking over to the bed as I placed the tea mug back on the nightstand.

"Jacob, this is too nice." I looked around the room, eying the fact that fresh, long-stem red roses were in a crystal vase on the nightstand. "You could've put me in a sleeping bag in the damn garage."

Jacob frowned as he sat in a corner chair between two bookshelves. It looked like a reading corner. I was definitely taking notes on how to redecorate my apartment. "That's no way to treat a lady in distress. You were in crisis. I had to get you somewhere comfortable."

"I-I get like that sometimes. I start having flashbacks, and I just black in and out. It usually happens when I'm alone or after

I'm done with one of those tricks. I don't even like sex," I admitted out loud for the first time.

Jacob sighed, sitting back in the chair. "Ya know, big bro Jacyn used to get like this. Moms sent us to swimming lessons. Jacyn used to be afraid of water, and Kelsius had nightmares every night about drowning. Neither of them talked during family therapy sessions. Afterward, they'd both go to their rooms and sit in their corners. Their worst meltdowns were on rainy days. One rainy day—I had to be about ten——I invited them both in my room to play Grand Theft Auto. Instead of turning on the game, I stepped outside on my balcony, out in the rain, and just laid down on the balcony floor. I let the rain hit me in the face. I mean it was *pouring* rain. I was drenched. I needed my brothers to know that water doesn't hurt. That storms are okay sometimes. They'd come lay out on the balcony with me. We'd lay there until the rain stopped, not saying a word."

I hesitated to ask, "Did it work?"

Jacob shrugged. "Kelsius still lays out on his patio on rainy days. He's still trying to process his emotions. Jacyn's mind found other ways to cope. You can say his mind is a little divided, literally. Grief reveals itself in different ways to different people. There's no one way to handle it. I think you're doing pretty well."

I laughed out loud. "Overdosing, fighting hospital staff, and about to blow my best friend's mother's head off is 'doing pretty well'?"

"You could've said fuck everyone and went right back to the club tonight. Instead, when I carried you inside, you laid right down in that bed and cried yourself to sleep," Jacob reminded me. "Baby steps. Oldest bro, Marcellus, is throwing a Halloween ball tonight. I promised I'd show my face, mingle with some guests that are joining Mom's choir. Not leaving you here alone, so shower and get dressed."

I definitely wasn't in the headspace to go out that night, but Jacob was being so hospitable. I took a shower, removed my damn lace front wig, washed and blow dried my hair. The nurse popped back up in my room, asking if I needed anything. I denied needing help, even though my hands were trembling. The moment I reached for the flat iron, she grabbed it and started ironing my hair. I hadn't cried in months like I cried that day. I hadn't received love like I was shown that day from anyone other than Mellie.

But the moment I entered that party, arm in arm with Jacob, all I felt was hate. The only one who came over to greet me was Kelsius. Everyone else at the party looked at me like I definitely didn't belong. There I was, minimal makeup, evening gown, high heels, hair flowing naturally down my back. Looking and feeling better than I'd ever felt when I was naked on stage. And everyone —especially the women—looked at me like I needed to get back on that stage where I belonged.

I went over to get a drink from the bar station when I remembered that I wasn't even supposed to be drinking. I asked for a Sprite. Two girls at the bar looked at me before talking to each other. They didn't even bother to whisper.

"Doesn't she work down at The Whore House?" the dark skinned one asked the brown-skinned one.

The brown-skinned one looked at me before pursuing her lips, and nodding. "Yeah, my brother calls her Peanut Butter, but I think her stage name is BeeBee or Big Back. I heard she was at a private party and let five men have sex with her, and she didn't even get paid. The club owner took the money, saying she owed her for the doctor's bills. They send their whores to the clinic every month to make sure they're clean to continue having sex with all their clients."

"You think your brother had sex with her?" The dark-skinned one looked at me before looking back at her friend.

"Yeah, he said he *and* his girlfriend had sex with her." The brown skinned one huffed.

I definitely remembered that situation. "Oh, your brother must be Teddy. I call him Teddy with the Tiny Penis. His girl was the reason I was there. We fucked, and *he* watched. I barely licked the nigga before he was nutting all over himself. Did he tell you he couldn't get it up to even fuck me? Niggas love telling my side of the story instead of telling their no-dick-having-ass side of the story."

"Maybe his penis isn't too small. Maybe your vagina is just too big, what's left of it anyway." The dark skinned one smacked her lips.

"What's your name? No, fuck that—what's your *nigga's* name?" I asked her.

She shook her head frantically. "No, baby, my man, Clinton Waters, is a man of God. He's a preacher's son. He's going to be a minister and—"

"He ate whipped cream from my ass at a bachelor party on top of a pool table." I cut her off. "Other than the Oxberry sons, there's not a nigga at the Oxberry Church who hasn't had his face between my ass."

Just went the brown-skinned girl was about to pull her friend out of the way to confront me for telling those hoes the truth, Lydia walked up to us.

"Ladies, are we having a good time?" Lydia faked a smile, looking at the two girls frowning at me before she observed the irritated expression on my face.

"Pastor Oxberry, you need to be careful who you invite to your church and be mindful of what type of trash your sons drag around with them." The dark-skinned chick pulled on her friend's arm, dragging her away from the bar station.

Lydia watched them walk away before she looked at me, taking a deep breath as she tried to calm herself. She was dressed like a character from the colonial ages. She looked like a *Bridgerton* extra. "I don't know what you're doing with my baby, Jacob, but he is a good man. Whatever he's doing for or with you, I have no idea. Jacyn is my adoptive son. What he does impacts this family, but not as much as my biological sons who have stake in my family's legacy. My son will not be romantically involved with a pretty prostitute."

I laughed out loud, gripping my cup in my hands and fighting every urge to toss that Sprite all over her face. "I didn't ask for any of this."

Lydia glared at me. "One of my guests manages that Charlotte rapper, The Entity. He asked Jacob about you, asking if you had a manager because they've seen you dance and wanted you to be one of the rapper's background dancers. Jacob told the man that he was your manager, and anything they wanted from you went through him first."

My eyes widened as my heart thumped in my chest.

"You're going to be trouble, I see." Lydia watched me shaking my head.

"I'm not trouble," I told the old bitch.

Lydia laughed a little, irritated by my presence in her world. "Ya know, your father, Tevin—"

I immediately corrected the bitch. "Umm, *step*father."

"Your *father*," she continued, "is good friends with the Biggs family. He told Scarlett's father that he was holding your mother's funeral this Sunday. I'll be giving a sermon on Jezebel that day. You'll get to hear my sermon from the first row while you view your mother's dead body. I saw her body down at the morgue. She was a beautiful woman."

"Watch it, Pastor Oxberry." I warned her to not get too comfortable with the disrespect.

The music changed from gospel to clean '90s R&B.

"Sorry didn't notice you then, but again you didn't notice me. But we'll remain passersby, until the next time we speak..." One of my favorite songs by Dru Hill "Beauty" interrupted me about to drench that petty bitch's face.

"Nah, *you* watch it," Lydia hissed. "Fuck with my son, and he'll be viewing *your* body from the first row." She walked past me, bumping my shoulder on the way.

I laughed, turning around to grab that bitch by her silver-streaked hair, when Jacob made his way over to me. My angry laughter faded as everything around me slowed down, and all I saw was that sexy-ass nigga strolling toward me.

"Can I have this dance?" he asked, eying a few couples go onto the dance floor to get a dance in. He looked back at me, biting his lip.

I wanted to say no, but he'd already grabbed my hand in his warm hand and led me toward the dance floor. The moment we reached the center, he turned to me, pulling my body against his, wrapping his hands around my waist, and gripping my dress.

My heart was beating so fast, and he felt it, too.

"Calm down, mamas." He laughed a little.

"I was about to drag *your* mamas," I snapped, eying the couples on the dance floor. Every woman was rolling her eyes at me. I shook my head, looking back up at Jacob, who was looking back down at me. "Your mama basically just called me a hoe and said if I fuck with her son, she was gonna put me in a pine box."

Jacob smiled a little. "No woman is good enough for her sons as far as she's concerned."

"I know I'm not your type. I'm not crazy enough to think I am, so your mama can chill the fuck out." I huffed, sliding my arms over his strong shoulders and wrapping my hands around his neck.

Jacob frowned a little. "Who says you're not my type?"

I pursed my lips at him. "Nigga, please. I've never seen you with a stripper-bitch."

"You've never seen me with *any* bitch." Jacob shook his head. "You know *of* me. You don't *know* me. There's a big difference. And why the fuck are you worried about what these boring ass women think about you? They wish they were you, which is why they're mad. You're most men's fantasy, and they're some nigga's boring reality. You represent something they can't be. That's all this is."

"You don't get it. It's not you they're talking shit about. Look," I let go of him, ruining our little slow dance, which would've actually felt really good under different circumstances, "I can't stay on your family compound."

Jacob agreed. "I can take you to my house in the mountains about two hours from here. I can get the nurse to stay out there with us. You could use two weeks in the mountains."

I hesitated. "And I'm not going to my mother's funeral. I kind of want to have my own ceremony for her. Just with close friends who I consider family. Could you set that up for me?"

Jacob nodded. "Yeah. But in the meantime, let's get away. We can get some sleep tonight, and head out in the morning."

* * *

One week at Jacob's place felt like a lifetime. I'd never been to Boone. His house was a four-bedroom cabin-style mansion which sat alongside a stream of water. I thought I was in paradise. No one for miles but us and nature. The nurse checked in twice that week, and called every day, three times a day, to make sure I was okay. Jacob worked for hours on end down in his basement, with a sign on the door that said, 'Do Not Disturb,' so I didn't. He'd make us breakfast, lunch, and dinner. I ate alone, while he ate in the studio.

He pretty much kept his distance until the night it rained cats and dogs. The nurse called and said she was stuck in Charlotte due to some roads flooding, and it wasn't safe to drive. I happened to walk past Jacob's bedroom door, which was open, when I noticed that the sheer curtains on his balcony entrance were swaying. When I went to close the doors, I spotted Jacob laid out on the balcony floor. Laid out there, no shirt, dark gray joggers.

I took a deep breath before I stepped outside.

Jacob looked up at me as I stood beside him in my bathrobe, rain already soaking into my clothes. I didn't care. It actually felt really good. The warm wind, the smell of the rain, the feeling of the rain against my skin. It was unusually warm for November and felt good all week. We hadn't had a good downpour, and I wanted to enjoy it. With him. So, I laid beside him.

We looked at each other before looking back up at the dark sky, closing our eyes as the water hit our faces. We lay there in silence. After about five minutes, the rain slacked a little.

I wiped the water from my face before saying, "I have a baby out there. I gave her up for adoption last year. She turned one today, November 7th."

"I have a son out there. He's four. I gave him up four years ago. His mother didn't want me to be his father."

I smacked my lips. "I bet she's probably married. You look like a homewrecker." I looked at him, realizing my joke wasn't funny to him. That my joke was his reality. "She *is* married, isn't she?"

Jacob didn't look at me. He continued to look up at the sky. "Not anymore, but I'm not the nigga she ever wanted. Just the nigga she needed for one night."

"She's fuckin' insane," I hissed. "Who wouldn't want you?"

"Her." He scoffed.

"Look, fuck her. Just get your son back. He's yours. You have rights," I tried telling him.

Jacob shook his head. "I wish it was that simple."

I had to get the subject off of him. I had no idea why he was laying out there in the rain, but I was sure my comment wasn't helping his mental state. I cleared my throat. "Ya know, I never had a boyfriend. I never even had sex that I actually enjoyed. Nobody has ever 'taken me through there.' I always got fucked like I was a whore. I don't feel like a whore when I'm around you."

Jacob finally looked at me, his bushed eyebrows knitting together. "The day we witnessed Jacyn and Melody's marriage ceremony, I peeped the look on your face. You want that shit. The man, the family, the love."

"I do, but that doesn't happen for women like me. Shit, why aren't *you* married? Look at all of this!" I looked at him as the rain stopped. "You-you're not still in love with that woman, are you?"

Jacob shook his head. "Nah. That ship has sailed and is never coming back. You were right when you said I was the spare. Marcellus inherits my family's recording company and their church building when my parents die. I only inherit their larger assets if something were to happen to Marcellus. I think even Jacyn gets shares of the record company. They even allowed Jacyn to keep the publishing rights of songs he wrote. My parent's company gets to license the songs that I write for ten years. I have to pay for songs that I produce to retain the masters, so you know they don't let me produce too many of their songs. My job in this family is to make sure everyone else is straight. I take care of everyone's problems while mine go unnoticed. I don't matter."

I disagreed. "You matter."

"To who?" Jacob wasn't trying to hear me.

"To me," I whispered. "Look at everything you've done for me. I'm so grateful. I've never been treated like this. I've never had anyone do anything for me unless I did something for them first. This is new. This is different. I know you're only doing this because your brother asked you to, but it still feels like the closest thing to love I've ever had."

"I was lonely for a long time before this. I might have done this for myself, too. Felt nice to take care of someone who actually appreciates me." Jacob sat up, getting up from the ground. He reached down to help me off the ground. "We should get inside. Get dry."

Jacob sat on a clean, plastic beige bench in his bathroom after he grabbed a few towels to dry off. Instead of drying himself off, he removed my damp robe, tossing it on the floor and eyeing my body in my drenched nightgown.

"Take this off," he demanded.

I pulled the gown over my head and tossed it on the floor alongside my robe. He started drying me off.

I stood between his legs, grabbing a towel to dry off his hair. I loved the fact that all the brothers had dreadlocks. Dreadlocks that they kept styled and maintained.

"Oh, I just love your hair. It's so dark and healthy. It's gonna frizz up in the morning. You gonna let me do your retwist?" I giggled a little, looking down into his face as he dried my legs off.

He wasn't saying a word, just taking his time drying me off.

I gasped as he pulled me down onto his lap. And he kissed me. The softest lips I'd ever felt. My first real kiss. A kiss that felt like someone cared and cherished me. A kiss that I wasn't expecting from someone like him. Stunned, I pulled away.

But he leaned in again to kiss me. That nigga made twenty more seconds feel like twenty more minutes. I held his face after we got a few strokes in. I pulled my lips from his, feeling like crying.

"I," I choked back the tears, "I don't deserve you. I don't deserve any of this. I appreciate everything, but I know this isn't reality. This beautiful life that you've shown me ends in a week. I know it ends once we get back to Charlotte, and we go our separate ways. You don't have to sell me a dream that I know is meant for someone else."

Jacob wasn't looking at my naked body. He was looking in my face. "You're safe here with me. You're safe in Charlotte with me when you get back."

"But I'm a hoe." I rolled my eyes, which started to water.

"The fuck do you think I've been doing?" Jacob asked. "I've been fuckin', too. That would make me a hoe, too. I don't give a fuck what you've done. As far as I'm concerned, your body count resets with me."

I did start crying then.

And he dried my tears, kissing my lips. "Baby steps, but you'll get there. I'll be right here with you."

That was the first night I slept with a man but didn't have sex with him. We lay on that bed, balcony doors open, and fell asleep to the sound of the stream outside the house. The weather lightened up the next day. The day that I chose for my mother's ceremony. I invited a few of the girls from the Midnight Ballet. And Mellie was there, helping set up the picture of my mother on the podium. I ran into my bestie's arms, crying. I hadn't seen her in about three weeks, and it felt like forever.

"What up, biihhhh?" Mellie laughed as I jumped in her arms, squeezing her as tightly as I could. As I let her go, she eyed Jacob walking into the room. She grinned at me, probably having a million questions about everything going on.

I started to ask her about her long trip to Europe, but then I spotted a pretty, brown-skinned girl talking to a few of my Strip Sisters. I frowned, nodding toward the pretty girl. "Who's that?"

Mellie's smile faded as she rolled her eyes a little. "Girl. Breelyn McNealson, this famous gospel singer. And my sister, apparently."

The bitch had *another* sister? My eyes widened. "What the fuck did I miss?"

"A lot." Mellie sighed heavily.

CHAPTER 8
Kelsius Bayou Simms

"Nigga, who invited this bitch?" I muttered, leaning back in my seat.

I sat at the back of the conference room at Oxberry Studios, the building where my adoptive family recorded, produced, and rehearsed their fake-ass praises to the God that they definitely didn't serve the way they claimed. Belle was remembering her mother that day in her own way, and Jacob was doing his part as whatever the fuck he was to her by organizing the remembrance of a woman who didn't deserve a funeral let alone a memorial service. And there Breelyn was, singing her pretty little heart out.

I couldn't even pretend it didn't hurt to see her, because it did. It had always been hard for me to show pain. It always came out in anger or frustration. I appeared and sounded angry to see Breelyn on that podium alongside Miss Ethel's portrait, but in actuality, I was hurt like a muthafucka.

Jacob frowned at me. "Nigga, who invited *you*?" he asked, nudging me as he slouched down beside me. He'd gotten up from the front row of the chairs he'd gathered around the podium to come and sit beside me at the back of the room. I was sitting by the fuckin' door, so I could leave as soon as the shit was the fuck over.

"Look, I'm just here for the ballerinas. Belle's Stage Sisters invited me to this party tonight. I'm their ride to the party, so they can ride a nigga *after* the party, you feel me?" I grinned a little, watching Jacob click his teeth.

"I thought you'd be happy to see your first love." Jacob smirked.

"I see you're not gonna be happy until I knock a few of your fuckin' teeth out," I snarled, ready to stand up from my chair and knock the nigga in the face with it.

Jacob was always fuckin' with me, typical big brother shit. He picked every opportunity to play with my emotions. Marcellus knew not to fuck with me. The last time he played with me by fuckin' this bitch I was involved with a few years back, I fucked that bitch in his recording studio before I burned millions of dollars' worth of equipment. Jacyn was too busy trying to protect me to do anything to trigger me. But Jacob enjoyed triggering a nigga every chance he got. Like he wanted to see how crazy I could get. He was like a fuckin' military training instructor. He loved to beat a nigga down, then try to build you back up in the same breath.

Truth was, I looked up to the stupid nigga. No matter how tough life got, no matter how hard everything was crumbling around him, Jacob always managed to keep it together. He could chop, screw, and mix any beat to any genre of music. His talent stretched beyond gospel, but he was always trying to impress his family. A family who focused most of their attention on their foster kids. Even though his parents focused their attention on me and Jacyn's emotional issues, Jacob still treated us like his biological brothers without letting jealousy get in the way. Of course he'd make jokes about me being his *not* brother, but it was all love.

Jacob was the only one who actually took the time to understand Jacyn's dual personality. Jacob's calming techniques became a part of my daily routine. Therapy was fuckin' pointless to me.

The amount of therapy that family paid for to get Jacyn and me the help they felt we needed, I'll never know. I don't think Lydia ever forgave herself for what she let happen to me in her home. And I never forgave her either. How could I, when her family's actions and her avoidance destroyed me into the man I am today?

I sat there in the back of that room, watching Breelyn singing one of her family's gospel songs from their "God's Connection" album. I missed that girl. I didn't remember how much I missed her until the weekend she showed up at my mother's church. It took everything in me not to go up to her the first day she popped up at the church, grab her, and kiss her, telling her how hard life had been without her. But you can't do the shit I did and expect forgiveness, even if it was eight years ago.

After the event, everyone chatted a little before heading their separate ways. I stood outside, smoking a Newport, leaning back along the cobblestone building. Jacob walked out of the sliding doors, alongside Belle. He glanced over at me before whispering to Belle that he'd catch up with her in a minute. He did that stupid smirk thing he did before walking over to me.

A few of the strippers that I was supposed to drive to their destination walked by, winking at me. They said they were going to ride with one of their homegirls, and that they'd text me the address to the party that was going on that night. The moment they said that shit, Breelyn came right behind them. She glanced at me and rolled her pretty brown eyes a little, putting her hands in her coat pockets as she strolled down the walkway toward the parking lot.

Jacob elbowed me. "You better catch up with her before her nigga comes to pick her up."

I made a face like I expected that beautiful brown woman to be single. "*What* nigga?"

"Her fiancé." Jacob snatched my cigarette and tossed it to the ground before he stepped on it to put out the flame.

"What fuckin' fiancé?" I questioned before looking back at Breelyn, who was slowly approaching her car.

"Science O'Kane," Jacob mentioned. He was about to explain how the two of them met, but I zoned out as soon as that name came out of his mouth.

Science O'Kane. That nigga was a quarterback for the Carolina Panthers. Twenty-three years old. Averaging $61 million a fuckin' year. The nigga had sports apparel lines and soul food restaurants distributed up and down the East Coast. There wasn't a celebrity party that didn't invite the nigga. The muhfucka completed an entire season with a fuckin' injured arm. His family attended the Oxberry church. He came from a Christian family that didn't believe in sex before marriage, so you never heard any groupie stories about the nigga. Either he paid the hoes off or that nigga was gay. That's why she was moving to Charlotte. To be closer to that gay ass nigga.

"Aye, girl," I called out as I approached her while she opened the driver's side door of her little white Lexus 350.

Breelyn turned around to face me, her curly, shoulder-length hair blowing in the wind. She had on a fluffy chocolate brown dress with a cropped jacket and stood about four inches off the ground in her pointy heels. She still had those cute moles on the side of her left eye and the prettiest brown eyes I'd ever seen. And that fuckin' chocolate skin looked so fuckin' lickable. I wanted to grab and kiss her, but I wasn't trying to scare her off. It had already been so long since I'd seen her.

I wish I hadn't hurt her the way I did. I was just so broken back then. I didn't have time for a fuckin' virgin. Shit, I still don't. And then they have the nerve to be some fine shit, too. What's the purpose of being fine if I can't stick dick in her? Get the fuck away from me. Fine, stingy pussy bitch.

"Aye, *boy*," she mocked, rolling her eyes and looking into my face.

I looked down at her, noticing the crystals she wore around her neck. The kids at school used to say she was a witch. She was into crystals, herbs, and healing. She used to light sage, and she even had a shrine in her room at her aunt's house. Everyone thought she was weird as fuck. I loved her weird. It shed some light on the darkness that I felt. I missed her so much.

"So, you moved to Queen City, huh?" I cleared my throat. I had no idea what I was even going to say to her. I was lucky she didn't slap me in the face.

"Yeah. It's easier to be closer to bae this way," she told me proudly. "All that flying out to see him every month is too much."

"How long have you been seeing this nigga?" I wanted to know.

She folded her arms. "We've been friends since high school. And we officially started dating about three years ago. He proposed to me on Valentine's Day." She showed me that big ass rock on her finger like I gave a fuck about that shit. She looked at her ring before looking up at the expression on my face. "What about you? Seeing anyone?"

I hesitated to answer the question when Belle's Stage Sisters approached in their car, rolling down the window.

"See you at the party tonight, Kelsius. Can't wait to choke on it." The freak with the split tongue and dermals stuck her tongue out before blowing me a kiss and darting out of the driveway. I couldn't remember her name. I just knew that fuckin' tongue of hers could do tricks that should be patented. I had her name saved in my phone as "Head Wrap."

Breelyn rolled her eyes from Head Wrap over to me. "Same old Kelsius, I see. I'm running a little late. I have to meet up with my homegirls to get things ready for my bachelorette party."

I don't know why that shit made my chest feel like it was caving in, but it did. "Bachelorette party?"

I guess she could sense that the shit bothered me. A stupid little sexy grin appeared on that pretty face of hers. "Yeah, we're getting married next week. At your mom's church on Saturday. My bachelorette party is next Friday."

I laughed a little, annoyed out of my fuckin' mind but trying to play the shit off. The shit wasn't supposed to hurt a nigga. I could have anyone I wanted. I don't know why hearing the fact that her wedding was right around the corner fucked with me. Maybe because in the back of my mind, she was the only girl I ever wanted. And I fucked that shit up. I was hurt, so of course I had to project.

"What's so funny?" Breelyn's eyebrows scrunched.

"Nothing. I just can't believe you're marrying a nigga named 'Science.'" I chuckled. "The nigga's parents definitely gave him the wrong name because he was definitely one of those kids the school system didn't leave behind. He only graduated because he had bitches doing his homework in high school. The coaches made sure he passed because scouts from all over the country wanted that nigga. He skipped over college football and went straight to the NFL. He might be slow, and his favorite color is fifteen, but he is fast out there on the field. I'll give your slow nigga that."

Breelyn faced me, looking up at me like she was finna tear a nigga the fuck down. "When I left my aunt's house that summer after eighth grade, Science flew all the way out to Houston to visit me. He came every month when my mama called and told him I couldn't eat, I couldn't sleep, I couldn't think without crying for *you*!" Breelyn shoved me in my chest as hard as she could. "That man resuscitated the life you took from me when you did what you did with my best friend! How you gonna talk shit about *my* man when you fucked a bitch named 'Delecia'?" Breelyn shoved me aside to reach for the door handle.

I grabbed her arm, sliding my hand down to her hand. "Breelyn, I'm—"

Breelyn looked in my face, her angry expression subsiding to hear what I had to say.

I wanted to tell her that I was sorry.

And just when she started to squeeze my hand back, I just had to say some stupid shit.

"I-I didn't know her name was Delecia. Y'all always called the bitch 'Cookie'." I barely got the shit out when Breelyn snatched away from me.

"Go to hell, Kelsius!" She huffed, pulling her car door open and jumping inside, slamming the door closed behind her.

I scratched my head anxiously as she burned rubber to get out of that parking lot and as far away from me as she could possibly get. And I couldn't blame her. I always caused more harm than good when it came to women. I can't tell you how many women I'd gotten pregnant within the past eight years of my life. The Oxberrys always paid the families of these girls off, paying for their abortion, even paying a few to stay the fuck away from me, which never worked.

Bonnie was the only one they couldn't pay off. The bitch couldn't wait to have a piece of me. My baby girl, Bayou, is the second love of my life. I had to pretend I wasn't attached to her just so Bonnie wouldn't try holding her against me. The games I had to play with women to keep the fuckin' peace was draining. It was my karma for what I did to Breelyn's peace.

My earliest memories of my life begin with Breelyn. Our mothers were what you would call frenemies. They were competing gospel singers. Lydia would have her songwriters write songs religiously dissing songs written by Carolina's song writer. Christian beef is real, I'm telling you, because I've seen some shady shit. I'd go to church just to see the drama as a kid. Me and my brothers would be dying watching them bitches snatch each other from the pews.

I remember meeting Breelyn during Sunday school the day of a gospel competition. I remember crying because I didn't want to stop playing with her when it was time to leave. Her aunt, Ms. Tanya, taught Sunday school at the Oxberry church. On holidays, Breelyn would come to town and stay with her aunt. I spent every Thanksgiving, Christmas, New Year, Easter, and summer vacation with Breelyn from pre-k all the way up until I was nine, when her aunt started dating Lydia's brother, Dawson.

Dawson was one of the only older male family members who took an interest in me as a kid. He took me fishing. Took me to boxing matches. Played basketball with me. Taught me how to tie my shoes. Taught me how to talk to girls. Took me out hunting. Taught me how to put up a tent, make a fire, treat insect bites. I thought of him as a father figure because Marcellus Senior worked so much that he was barely home. Dawson came over every day to pick me up. Pick *only* me up. And no one thought anything of it because he was one of the deacons at the church. He did everything he had to do to gain my trust.

Then, out of nowhere, Dawson broke that trust when he broke me on the floor of my bedroom. I kicked and screamed and tried to use every ounce of strength I had in my nine-year-old body to fight the nigga from ripping my striped pajamas off. The family was supposed to be gone to a gospel convention, when Marcellus Senior happened to come into my room to look for Jacob's tie that Lydia forgot to pack and thought she may have mixed it up with my laundry.

My adoptive father tried to kill that nigga that day. And he would have had Lydia not stopped him and called the police on her brother. I later found out that Dawson was killed in jail. Tanya didn't even want to know what happened the day Dawson was arrested. She just said fuck the nigga once he went to jail.

The family did everything they could to keep what happened to me sealed from the public. They didn't want it to "taint" the church. And that's when something in me changed. I felt like I didn't matter. I didn't feel like a man. I didn't feel like my body even belonged to me. I needed to erase that feeling. I was told by my family therapist that I needed to come out of my room and try socializing again with my peers. I went over to one of my classmates' houses. His sixteen-year-old sister was there. I was left alone in the house with her. She said her mother was on the phone talking to her friend who's a cop about what happened to me. She said she was sorry and could make me feel better if I needed her to. One thing led to another, and she made me feel better alright. Made me forget being pinned to the floor by a muthafucka who I looked up to.

I never talked to Breelyn about what I'd been through. I kept that shit bottled. I didn't want to bother her with my trauma. I just wanted her to have the best parts of me. She was so giggly, goofy and sweet. That's how I wanted things to stay with us. Uncomplicated. It was her who asked me to my eighth-grade dance. She stayed with her aunt during our eighth-grade year.

The night that I was supposed to take her, I walked past Lydia's office, overhearing her on the phone telling Breelyn's aunt about what her brother did to me. Explaining what happened the day the nigga was arrested and what Marcellus Senior caught her brother doing to me. I'd put those memories away for four years, and there they were, coming back to haunt me.

I ended up calling off our date and went with another girl, Breelyn's best friend, who I knew would give up the pussy. Delecia was the total opposite of my sweet Breelyn, who wouldn't even kiss a nigga. Once Breelyn found out, she never spoke to me again, and that was eight years ago.

* * *

"*Fuck*," I muttered as I pressed the buttons on the keypad entry to my house, only for it to alert me that the battery had died.

I needed to get into my stash. My anxiety was through the fuckin' roof. Jacyn and the virgin he broke in were on a double date with Jacob and Bonnie, or some shit. I didn't want to bother either of them with my bullshit, when they were actually happy and enjoying life for once. Both of them had spare keys to my back door. The only other spare key was in a lockbox in my adoptive parents' mansion across the acres of land they owned.

I hoped I could get into the lockbox under the kitchen sink without running into Lydia. But the moment I went into the mansion, she was hanging up her coat on the coat tree in the hallway. She grinned a little when she saw me, probably happy to see me, but her smile quickly faded when she saw the expression on my face, which let her know that I was far from happy to see her bitch ass.

She cleared her throat "Kelsius."

"Lydia," I responded, walking around her through the vestibule to enter the enormous living area. "I got locked out of my place. Just coming over to get the spare key."

"Oh, okay." Lydia followed far behind me, knowing to keep her fuckin' distance. "I'm just getting back from the church. Ummm, they're making sure that everything is good for next week. For Breelyn's wedding."

"Uh-huh." I walked toward the kitchen, which smelled like it was drenched in lemon Pine Sol and bleach. Lydia fired the last housekeeper who left a fingerprint on her Bosch stainless steel stove. The new housekeeper made sure every maid who worked on the premises didn't so much as leave a piece of dust on anything. Lydia had a way of making everyone around her feel fuckin' uncomfortable.

"She's looking for a wedding singer." Lydia approached the kitchen as I bent down to grab the lockbox. "Remember when you used to sing at the church with your brother? You had one of the strongest voices in the choir at such a young age. Oh, people would travel from across the country to hear the little boy with the voice of an angel! You haven't sang in the church since you were nine and—" She stopped talking.

I paused before standing up to place the lockbox on the counter.

"We're having dinner tonight with Breelyn's mother and aunt. You're welcome to come." Lydia approached the island, standing across from me as I opened the lockbox.

"You know Carolina can't stand a nigga," I mumbled, opening the lockbox and digging through it for my key.

"I know you didn't mean to hurt her." Lydia said something I didn't expect her to say.

I looked up at her, my heart racing.

"It wasn't your fault what Dawson did to you, Kelsius." She just kept on fuckin' digging into my wounds.

"Then whose fault was it? Yours? For keeping the shit a secret to protect your family's reputation?" I snatched my key from the box.

"He's dead, Kelsius! What else do you want from me?" Lydia exclaimed. "I know everyone thinks it was Senior who had him killed, but... it was me. I knew someone in jail from the Biggs family. I promised him I'd get him a better lawyer if he had someone inside kill my brother. You were just a little boy, and—"

"So, you want a medal? You want the Congressional Medal of Honor or some shit for protecting that little boy a little too fuckin' late?" I grabbed the box and tossed the shit back under the sink without even locking it back. Keys went flying everywhere.

"I'm *still* protecting that little boy!" Lydia screamed back. "You live on *my* property where I pay every single bill! You don't have and won't go out there and get a job! You wouldn't go to college! Your clothes, your cars, the weed you fuckin' smoke, the food you feed to those bitches who sneak across the lawn every other night—all that shit is paid for by me and your fuckin' father! If I didn't care about you, you wouldn't be here! If I didn't love you, I wouldn't have taken you into my home and raised you for the last fuckin' twenty-one years! I'm sorry for what my evil brother did to an innocent little boy! But he' gone!"

"But the pain isn't," I admitted, feeling pressure in my chest.

Lydia's eyes swelled with tears. "I know, baby."

"When does it stop?" I asked her.

Lydia dried her face. "Baby, I don't know the answer to that one."

The doorbell rang.

Lydia watched as one of her maids hurried down the spiraling staircase to answer the door. Just when the day couldn't get any fuckin' worse, Bonnie stomps her stupid ass inside the house, yelling like Bow Wow's baby mama in that Tyler Perry movie. You know what fuckin' movie I'm talking about.

"Kelsiusssss! Nigga, where the fuck are you?" Her voice echoed through the house as she walked into the living room and spotted me standing across from Lydia at the counter. She was holding our baby in her arms.

Bayou started bouncing up and down in her arms as soon as she spotted me in the kitchen. I walked around the island as Bonnie put our baby down, and she ran her little bow-legged ass into my arms.

That shit made my heart smile. My little baby was so cute and bubbly. Her brown skin, her little curly Afro puffs, her fat cheeks. That little girl could eat. She had dimples everywhere. She was fifteen months and eating everything we ate. Steak, lobster, oxtails, shrimp, goat, potatoes, everything. You'd call her name, and she would act like she didn't hear you. Let you open a bag of Cheese Puffs, and her little fat ass would come running.

"Bayou-baby!" I laughed as she hugged me around my neck, her chubby arms damn near strangling me. "Damn, Avenger! You about to choke ya daddy!"

Lydia giggled, drying her face before looking at Bonnie's irritated expression. Lydia's smile faded as she rolled her eyes. "You said you'd be here at 8:00. It's early, honey, and I have a lot to cook tonight for a family dinner."

"Well, I have shit to do tonight, too." Bonnie smacked her lips, tossing her hair over her shoulder. "My lil cousin is in town, and I gotta take her shopping for some bachelorette party she's planning for her friend, who's getting married at your church next weekend. That little gospel princess."

I frowned, wanting to ask more, but I didn't. I just took my baby over to the fridge and got her an apple juice. I was hoping Lydia would continue asking questions, so I could pull up on shawty.

Lydia glanced at me before looking at Bonnie, who was looking at me. "Oh, yeah, Breelyn is getting married next Saturday. Her bachelorette party is next Friday. Where is it again?"

Bonnie looked at Lydia, squinting as if trying to figure out why Lydia was asking questions. "Ummm, at that black owned skating rink called Inline in Midtown. Around 6:30. I don't know the girl; not my crowd. A bunch of preacher's kids. Everyone invited is young and married. Anyway, yeah, I gotta take her shopping, and you know Bayou cries for everything in the store."

"So," I handed my baby a box of animal cookies as I lowered her to the floor. "I pay you $1800 a month in child support, which you don't fuckin' need."

"Correction," Bonnie snapped. "Your *mama* pays me $1800 a month in child support! You don't even have a fuckin' job. Your job is living off your family's money!"

"Jacyn's practice is opening the week of Thanksgiving," Lydia interjected. "He's the office manager, if you must know. He has a job."

"And I bet he'll be fuckin' all Jacyn's clients." Bonnie scoffed.

"Can you not talk that way around Bayou?" Lydia exhaled sharply. "You can go about your business, Bonnie. I'll watch my grand baby."

Bonnie rolled her eyes from Lydia over to me. "Can we talk outside for a minute?"

I didn't want to talk to the bitch, but I knew she wasn't leaving unless I gave her some sort of conversation. Just about every night she'd pick a fight with me, thinking that shit would stop me from going out. I was supposed to go out with the Ballerinas from the club, but I wasn't in the mood for shit after actually getting the chance to talk to Breelyn. I had to figure out a way to get to her, talk to her, explain some shit to her.

As soon as I stepped out onto the front porch, Bonnie was running her fuckin' mouth. I just leaned back against one of the pillars and lit a fuckin' cigarette.

"How the fuck can you let Jacyn marry a bitch you had your dick up in?" Bonnie hissed in my face.

I just looked at the bitch like she was crazy. "I didn't fuck that bitch. If I did, promise you, she'd be just as delusional as you are. Nothing happened between us. I told you that shit. Stay out of that shit. Let Scarlett handle her own problems. Be mad at herself and those doctors who misdiagnosed her. Don't be mad at my brother for doing exactly what the fuck she told him to do." I pulled from the cigarette.

Bonnie looked my face over. "What are you doing tonight?"

"Not you." I exhaled smoke from my mouth and nose.

"Then who, nigga?" Bonnie shoved me in my shoulder.

"Put your hands on me one more time, and I will toss your muthafuckin' ass in these rose bushes," I warned her.

"What bitch you fuckin' tonight? I heard you were going to that party tonight at Drop Top. Those bitches slobber on dicks every fuckin' night! How many STDs have you given me, Kelsius? I'm just lucky that I've caught shit that there's antibiotics for!" Bonnie hollered, getting even angrier because her words weren't fazing me.

"You could always leave me the fuck alone. Move on. Fuck another nigga reverse cowgirl. Suck another nigga's dick from the back. I'm sure there's some nigga out there who's never *ever* had that happen to him. Let him see what that shit feels like." I thought about the shit myself when I said it.

That girl could pull my dick to the back of her throat, just using her throat muscles. No hands. The first time she did that shit, I wanted to strangle her. I had PSTD, and anything back in that area was a trigger. I had therapy as a child to even be able to wash my ass after what that muthafucka did to me. Bonnie was the only woman I'd been with who'd lick every inch of my body. And I do mean every inch. Everyone thinks they'd had a freak until they had one. I was drunk when she licked my balls, sliding her tongue between my ass to lick my asshole, too. I'd let her lick the muthafucka, but I would've kicked her in her face if she thought she was gonna stick anything in a nigga.

"That's all I am to you, Kelsius? Just sex?" Bonnie asked me that question every time she saw me. Not a day went by that we didn't have the 'what are we' talk. Everything I'd ever said to her would go in one ear and out the other. I needed to leave that crazy bitch alone.

"Have we ever gone on a date? Have we ever gone out to eat?

To a movie? The only reason you even know my family is because we have a baby together. I'm not even the kind of nigga your parents want to see you with. Your mama can't stand a nigga, and your father said he'd hide my body in one of the morgues that his family owned if I thought I was going to let you raise our daughter by yourself," I reminded her. "We fuck each other when we're fucked up. The only reason I let you stay over is because I can't let my baby's mama drive drunk. As soon as the sun comes up, I put your ass out. We don't cuddle. We don't kiss. You've never heard me say that word that starts with 'L,' and you won't ever hear me tell you that shit. I don't wanna be with you, and I put that on every muthafuckin' thing I fuckin' own. On my fuckin' mama."

She knew I was serious when I said that shit. I never brought up the mama I wish I would've gotten the chance to know. That was another burden of guilt I carried. That my birth is what killed her. That my birth is the reason Jacyn's mind was split in two. I killed our mother. And that caused a chain reaction to the other catastrophic shit in our lives.

"You don't mean that shit." Bonnie's eyes watered. "You don't be talkin' all this shit when you're in this pretty pink pussy. You love this pretty pussy, and you know it!"

She was right. I did love that pussy. Shit, I loved pussy period. The more of it I got, the more of it I wanted. It was like a fuckin' drug. But the moment Breelyn showed her face back in Charlotte after eight years, I realized it wasn't pussy that I craved. It was something so much deeper than pussy.

"Get the fuck on, Bonnie," I told the bitch as my iPhone chimed in my pocket.

I pulled it out to peep the text. It was my homeboy, Reddick. Known the nigga since elementary school. His family owned a security company. Anyone who was high profile hired them to do security detail at their parties. When I wanted to get into any party I wasn't supposed to be at, I'd get in touch with Reddick.

Bonnie was running her fuckin' mouth, and I was tuning the

bitch out until she snatched my fuckin' phone. "Nigga, listen to me when I'm fuckin' talkin' to you! Who is this bitch that's got you ignoring me the past two and a half weeks? Everything you do to her, I'm gonna have a nigga do to you!"

That shit triggered the fuck out of my PTSD. I tossed my cigarette before I snatched my fuckin' phone back from her, then grabbing her by her neck and slamming her into the pillar behind her.

"The fuck did you just say to me, bitch?" I snarled in her face, watching her giggle until I squeezed a lot harder, cutting off her circulation. "Say something now, muthafucka. You gonna get a nigga to do *what* to me? Keep talking all that shit. I got something for all that fuckin' mouth you got!"

The door flew open, and Lydia came flying out. She already knew what time it was when Bonnie came over and wanted to talk. Talking either turned into us fighting on the front porch or us fuckin' on the front porch. There was no in between with us.

"Kelsius, no!" Lydia ran up on us, snatching Bonnie from me.

Bonnie gasped for air as she grabbed her neck, looking at me like she couldn't believe I'd put my hands on her for the 50-11th fuckin' time. "Muthafucka, you gonna pay for putting your fuckin' hands on me!"

Fattie Bayou came running out the front door, attempting to run over to me when Bonnie rushed over and snatched her up. Bayou let out a scream, reaching for me as Bonnie hurried off the porch steps.

"Bonnie, I thought you were leaving her here!" Lydia called out to Bonnie as she raced down the walkway.

"Bitch, *fuck* you and *fuck* that son who you should've let drown during Hurricane Katrina with his fuckin' mama! Would've saved the world from another fuck nigga!" Bonnie cried and screamed at the same time. "I'm never gonna bring my baby back over here!"

"Yes, you will, bitch." I laughed, leaning back against the pillar, about to text Reddick back and see what he was up to. I needed to get fuckin' high. I needed to forget my fuckin' life for a few hours.

Lydia shoved me in my chest. "That girl is gonna be the death of you. I've been teaching you the three Ps all your lives! Say it with me."

I huffed. "'All pretty pussy isn't penetrable.' Damn, Lydia. You don't think I regret fuckin' that crazy bitch?"

Both of us watched Bonnie run over Lydia's favorite rose bushes.

"Whew, lord Jesus!" Lydia screamed. "Let me go inside and get my bible. I need to pray before I kill this bitch." She huffed before turning around to go back inside.

CHAPTER 9
Kelsius

"What's up, dawg?" Reddick dapped me up the following Friday night outside of Inline. He glanced at me before looking at all the Christian Cuties waiting in line to get their barcodes scanned to enter the skating rink for Breelyn's bridal shower.

All the little cuties were checking a nigga's drip out. Dressed in all black from my hat to my Red Bottom sneakers. Even my jewelry was black chrome and black diamonds. I had to wear all black to attend the funeral shower. I mean, the bridal shower.

"Don't cause a scene, nigga," Reddick warned me as he unhooked the velvet rope, letting me cut in front of everyone.

Soon as I walked through the skating room, I knew I would have to go to the DJ booth. Didn't nobody wanna hear no fuckin' Beyoncé. How the fuck was anyone supposed to dance to that shit? A few of my niggas escorted some of the church chicks (or what we liked to call Bible Bitches) to the party. Had to make sure I wasn't at that muthafucka by myself in case Science got wind that I'd shown up. He did pay for the entire rink to be rented out for bae's bridal shower. Reddick let me know Science was in Raleigh at his bachelor party. I had a couple of girls from

Midnight Ballerina slide through to distract him while I distracted his not-so-future wife.

Couples were scattered throughout that muthafucka, skating and dancing. I spotted Breelyn over by the concession stand, sitting in a throne-like seat. Presents on a table alongside her. She had a glass of champagne and looked bored out of her mind. She looked like a woman who overplayed her part so much that she didn't even want to play it anymore. Reddick ran in the celebrity circles, sports celebrities, specifically. He'd heard things about Science. Said the nigga had a chick on the side. I didn't question him because there was dirt on every celebrity. You never knew what was real or what was gossip. But that look on Breelyn's face definitely wasn't happiness. More like "let's wrap this shit up."

I approached the DJ booth, dapping him up. DJ Wraith worked with Jacob on a few of the songs he'd produced without his parents' knowledge. He looked bored out of his mind playing that soft R&B, censored shit. He looked happy to see a nigga, knowing I was gonna turn shit up a few notches for the ladies. The crew that matched with a few of the ladies from Breelyn's party were part of a professional skate team. As soon as the DJ switched songs, they were on their feet, headed to the rink to put in the footwork. Once the beat dropped, the lights in their wheels flashed like club lights.

That light in Breelyn's eyes was all I needed. It was our song. A song we used to get in trouble for singing in the car on the way to gospel conventions. She grinned, holding her champagne glass in the air as she watched the skate team fuck it up on the dance floor. I grinned, thanking bro for putting on something to liven the party up a little. Let the little bible baddies let loose. It wasn't Sunday, shit. Let the little hoes sin a little, ya know?

I stepped down from the DJ booth, watching out for the cuties skating by and making their way out onto the dance floor. "Post up on the whip and start lookin' for somethin' bad. Nice thighs, cute face, and gotta have a fat ass. Bust that pussy open then I tell her bring it back..." I sang along with the music, making my way toward the concession stand where Breelyn was sitting in her chair, looking so pretty.

Breelyn wore a tight, knee-length white dress that had one sleeve. Her hair was braided to one side. Red lipstick painted her full, pouty lips. She drank from her glass, leaving a thick lipstick smudge. Her eyes followed my steps as I approached her. She lowered her glass, taking a hard gulp as I sat on the bench of the table that had all those expensive gifts. I sat a few feet away from her to put some distance between us, when I really wanted her in my fuckin' lap, so I could squeeze on her a little. I just wanted to touch her.

Both of us just watched as my crew had the girls screaming their names. Breelyn looked out onto the skating rink floor, gazing as if she remembered a time when she used to skate. A time when we used to skate together. We damn near spent every day at that skating rink during the holidays that she stayed with her aunt. At one time in her life, she wanted to be a professional ice skater or a gymnast. She was actually pretty good. At skating and at bending her body in ways that made me wanna bend her the fuck over. Though we weren't speaking to each other in that moment, it felt good to just be in her presence and breathe the same air as she was breathing. We spoke without speaking. I found myself getting lost in the words she didn't even have to say.

Once she started applauding her girls being scooped onto the dance floor, that was my cue to speak. She was in a good mood at that moment, so maybe she wouldn't cuss a nigga out too bad. Shit, I was lucky she didn't kick a nigga the fuck out on sight, and fire security for letting me the fuck in.

I cleared my throat. "You look good, mamas."

She smacked her lips, her smile fading as she rolled her eyes from her friends who were enjoying themselves to me, a nigga who wasn't invited. "I know," she hissed.

"Ya mama came over the crib last week for dinner. She didn't say one word to me. She's still that same bitch she's always been." I leaned forward, resting my forearms on my thighs, looking out at the skate floor. "She never liked a nigga. Does she like Algebra? How do they get along?"

"Her and *Science* get along just fine, thank you," she corrected me.

"How do *you* and Science get along? Is he good to you?" I asked her.

Breelyn looked at me like I'd lost my fuckin' mind. "He treats me better than you did."

"I'd hope so. I was thirteen. I didn't know any better." I frowned, eyeing a shawty who was skating past the wall. She gasped when she saw me sitting there talking to Breelyn. I didn't know the bitch, but she looked familiar like a muthafucka. I shook it off and looked back at Breelyn.

"And you still don't know any better." She scoffed, fidgeting with her long braids. "You still play with hearts because you don't have one. You're emotionless. You don't feel anything for any of these women you sleep with. You even have a daughter. Do you love her?"

"My heart stopped beating June 26th, 2019, and didn't start beating again until August 10, 2025." I told her. June 26th 2019 was the last time I saw Breelyn. August 10, 2025 was the year Bayou was born.

"Why are you even here, Kelsius? I'm getting married tomorrow." Breelyn had to remind me of that bullshit.

"I just wanted to talk to you before became Mrs. Byron Douglas," I joked, referring to one of her favorite '90s show, *A Different World*.

Breelyn rolled her eyes, looking back out at the dance floor at her friends having a great time. "I'm supposed to be out there having a good time with the bridal party, but I'm sitting here with you."

"You were sitting here before I even showed up, mamas. Don't blame that shit on me." I made a face. "You miss me. I get it, though."

Breelyn looked back at me, watching me grin. "Boy, I do *not* miss anything about you."

I disagreed. "You do. If you didn't, you would've had security kick me the fuck out."

Breelyn took the last few sips from her champagne. "I knew that you know the men Science hired as security for this party. I guess he forgot that you all went to school together, but I didn't. The way Reddick runs his mouth, I knew you'd find me."

"So, you were waiting for me to show up?" I couldn't help but smile at that shit.

"Oh, my goodness, is that Kelsius?" A voice from a female who was there to start some shit approached me to my left.

I peeped the irritated expression on Breelyn's face before I looked over my shoulder to see her old best friend, Delecia, standing there, grinning from ear to ear. It didn't surprise me that she'd show up to the party. The way Breelyn's mama glared me down that night Lydia invited her for dinner, I knew she'd invite someone to her daughter's party to remind her how much of a fuck-nigga I was.

"What's up?" I nodded at her before turning my attention to Breelyn, who was gripping that empty champagne glass like she wanted to throw that shit at my face.

"It's been what, eight years?" she squealed. "You look so good! And you're a dreadhead? Aye, loc gang!" She shook her shoulder length dreds.

"You're not really considered part of the gang if you have loc extensions, are you?" Breelyn pretended to be thinking about the answer to that question before she rolled her eyes at Delecia.

Delecia rolled her eyes. "Anyway, Breelyn, congratulations. Your mama invited me to your party and your wedding. I'm guessing my invitation got lost in the mail. I know you're not holding a grudge from middle school, boo. You moved on to bigger and better, trust me."

Breelyn laughed, getting up from her chair. "Yeah, and how

do you know I moved on to 'bigger and better'? Did you have sex with my fiancé, too?"

I stood from the bench, blocking Breelyn's access to hit that girl in the face with that glass. That was the last thing Breelyn needed with cameras around. The moment I stepped inside the place, I saw a few iPhones flashing. Muthafuckas couldn't do shit without taking a fuckin' picture.

"We were kids, Breelyn! Got damn!" Delecia huffed.

"I don't give a fuck! He was mine!" Breelyn pushed me out of the way to get to Delecia, but I snatched her back. "Get the fuck off of me, Kelsius!" She pulled away from me. "Both of you, get the fuck out before I have security drag you both out of here by those fuckin' dreds!"

Breelyn stormed off toward the bathroom. I knew better than to go after her, and so did Delecia. Delecia threw her hands up and walked away from the failed attempt to reunite with her friend. I knew she needed to cool off. If Delecia hadn't shown the fuck up, I would've had her right where I wanted. I stepped outside the place, but I didn't leave. The party would be over in about two hours. I went around the corner to a bar, had a few drinks, came back to my car, and waited for her to come out.

Around 9:00, the party was over. The cleanup crew that was hired made their way in while Breelyn, her bridal party, and guests were making their way out. A limo was supposed to arrive to take the bridal party back to the hotel where they were supposed to get ready for the wedding the next morning. They all looked around for the limo that was supposed to be waiting at the end of the red carpet. The limo that I told to leave, so I could take bae home myself. I didn't give a fuck how the other bitches got back to the hotel, but she was going with me.

I sat in my car, watching as two Uber XLs pull up. The ladies were helping Breelyn put her gifts into the SUVs. I put the car in drive, making my way over to the cars just as they were about to load the last few gifts into the trunk. I pulled behind the second car and got out.

"I got you," I told Breelyn as I approached her, taking the few boxes that she had in her arms from her.

"We're heading to the hotel, Kelsius." One of her cousins, Naiomi, spoke up, frantically shaking her head at Breelyn before looking at me like I'd lost my mind even approaching her cousin. "We have to get up bright and early to get my cousin into that wedding gown. And right after the wedding, she's flying to Japan with her husband while he signs these endorsement deals with a few designer clothing lines. She doesn't have time to reminisce with you. Aren't you usually throwing fifties onto the stage at the Midnight Ballerina on Fridays?"

Breelyn looked at her cousin as she mumbled to herself while getting into the car.

"We can't fit all these boxes in the trunk, ma'am," the driver from the first Uber called out to Breelyn. "I'm just going to set them aside, so I can get your friends to the hotel."

"No way we're fitting all this stuff in here either." The other driver told the rest of the girls the same thing as they tried to squeeze more stuff into the trunk.

Breelyn exhaled deeper. "I'll have to take this stuff to the condo."

I looked at her. "Like I said, I got you."

"She's been drinking, Kelsius," Naiomi called out from the car like I couldn't see that Breelyn was stumbling a little. "Drop that stuff off and then bring her right over. She hasn't even shown any of us her new place. You don't need to be over there either. Drop her stuff off, then bring my cousin to us."

That bitch always got on my fuckin' nerves. She used to babysit us when we were younger and never gave us any fuckin' snacks. Her mama's house was always hot as fuck, and they had those fuckin' plastic covers on their shit. Shit that shouldn't have even still been around in the fuckin' 2000s. Who the fuck still had plastic on their furniture in 2010? *Her* damn fat ass mama and mean ass grandma. Her grandma was always whuppin' us with a Kool-Aid spoon when we'd steal cookies and shit. That day they put that old bitch in a home, I was standing out on the lawn, smiling from ear to fuckin' ear.

"A'ight," I responded, having no intention of dropping that girl back off at whatever fancy hotel they were staying in for the night. I helped Breelyn into the passenger seat before I loaded the rest of her gifts into my car.

* * *

"This shit is nice." I admired shawty's new place after bringing the last set of gifts into her condo and placing them on her glass dining room table. Her condo was on the third floor of the 8-story apartment building. The shit was laid out like a penthouse suite at a luxury hotel. Everything in that muthafucka was powder pink. "The nigga let you decorate, I see."

"'Let me decorate'?" Breelyn giggled. "Boy, this is *my* place," she corrected me as she went over and slid the blinds back on the sliding glass doors in her living room to reveal her roof-top view. "I bought this place for myself. I'm keeping this place while I move into one of his mansions. I may just rent this place out. Or come here whenever that mansion gets lonely while he's away on business trips." She fumbled a box she had in her hands, dropping it on the floor.

I looked up at her, watching her pick up some lingerie that fell out of the box. "Let me see that shit," I said, walking over to her.

She held up the black lace bra and panties, having a look for herself.

I eyed the black garter belt and tights that were on the ground before looking back at the lace she held in her hands. "Freaked out church muthafuckas," I commented.

"So, married Christians can't have sex?" Breelyn huffed, pushing past me and taking her little slutty outfit with her. "All my friends who gave me these gifts are married."

"Happily?" I turned toward her, watching her stumble over to that pink plush couch to have a seat.

"Look at this gift." She avoided the question as she opened a small box on the table.

I frowned, walking over to the table as soon as I saw something sparkling from inside the box. A closer view of the box revealed there were three stainless steel butt plugs in three different sizes in the box. The top of each one was a white heart. I watched Breelyn take one out of the box and press the heart, and the muthafucka started flashing different colors.

"Aye, yoooo." I laughed a little, shocked to see my sweet girl with shit like that.

"Shit, if these women aren't happy, I know their husbands are!" Breelyn giggled a little, watching me sit down next to her, taking the plug from her hands. "And this is the *small* plug!"

"You gonna let the nigga put this shit up your ass, Breezy?" I called her by her nickname.

"I don't know. I might walk around with it for a couple of hours to get used to it, ya know?" Breelyn peeped the disgusted look on my face as I hurried up and put that shit back in the box.

"Yeah? Well, I hope you shit on yourself," I muttered as she laughed out loud. "What other type of freaked-out shit do you have in these boxes?"

Breelyn smiled sheepishly. "You *sure* you want to see?"

I just looked at her.

She exhaled sharply before reaching for another box. She opened it, holding it up for me to read the fuckin' name on the box.

"'Cyber Milking and Stroking Masturbator'?" I took the box from her hands and read the description on the box. 'Use both hands to steer your pleasure as the phone mount holds your phone... Enjoy three speeds and seven speeds of vibration combined with six stroking modes.' This shit even heats up! They got your man a mechanical pussy?"

"Ugh." Breelyn snatched the box away from me, putting it back in the gift box. "It's for when he's away, and we have phone sex, or when he's home, and I'm too tired for it. Or when we have a baby, and my six weeks aren't up. It's so... he doesn't think he needs anyone else but me."

I looked at her as she fidgeted anxiously with her hair. "A male vibrator isn't gonna stop a nigga from cheating. He'll take that toy with him to the other bitch's house."

"We also got," she changed the subject, "kitchenware, bed clothes, baby clothes..."

I looked at her. "You're pregnant?"

Breelyn made a face. "No. His mama keeps hinting at the fact that she wants grandchildren."

"Is that what you want? To have the nigga's baby?" I asked her.

"You know," Breelyn laughed to herself. "I think I watched every type of porn there is. Anal porn. Lesbian porn. Gay porn. Threesomes. Gang bangs. I studied the positions. Practiced my arch so I'd know how to hold it when the time was right. Did my squats everyday so I wouldn't get tired after a few bounces on top. I spend an hour on the stairmaster a day to keep my cardio up. I drink water. I take probiotics. I don't use scented products down there. I wax every six weeks. I got a little bunny rabbit tattooed on my left butt cheek! And last week, I went and got a VCH!"

I made a face. "What's that?"

"A vertical clit hood piercing! I have a barbell going through my clit hood, vertically!" she exclaimed. "All this for my wedding night! I wanted my first time to be——"

I cut her off. "Hold up. First time? You haven't fucked this nigga yet, and y'all have been dating *how* long?" Oh yeah, that nigga was definitely fuckin' other bitches.

"I'm too drunk right now to talk about this." Breelyn huffed, removing her coat and draping it across the arm of the chair. "Let's talk about you, and why you don't have a girlfriend." Breelyn reached in her purse, pulling out what looked like a Ziplock bag of ten tubes of grape juice.

"What's that?" I asked as she handed me two.

"Taylor Port mixed with Henny." She smiled, popping the top from one of the tubes and tossing it back.

"I thought you wanted me to drop you off at the hotel," I reminded her.

She rolled her eyes. "I can have an Uber drop me off in a few if we get too drunk. And you can call your brothers if you have to. I haven't seen you in eight years. You can't sit and talk for a little while, Kellz?"

Shit, after drinking all ten of those tubes, neither of us could barely talk without laughing. On top of the drinks I had at the bar, and the drinks she had at her party, we were no good. Sitting there laughing about our childhood felt really good. It had been a minute since I actually sat down and talked to a woman about the best parts of life. The part of life before things got complicated and dark. I had nightmares just about every night of drowning. I'd wake up coughing like I just came up from under water, gasping for air. In those dreams, all my brothers were drowning. Breelyn was in those dreams, too, only she was above the water, reaching in to try to save me, but I couldn't reach her hand.

"So, you remember when we stopped up my grandma's toilet with my Barbie clothes?" Breelyn laughed. "And put mouthwash in the toilet! When she got home from work, she was like, 'The hell is that minty smell?' We were like, 'we're in here washing clothes!'"

I chuckled a little. "Yeah, I remember the way she beat our asses with that switch, too. I think she made my mama pay for the plumber. She just knew that shit was my idea." I watched her laughing, leaning forward to finally unbuckle her shoes after about two hours of talking about the good old days. I stopped her from unbuckling her shoes so I could do it for her. "I love the way your toenails shine. They look 3D and shit."

She giggled. "They match my stiletto nails, too. It's called cat eye nails."

"Pink is still your favorite color I see." I admired her toes as I removed her shoes, placing them under her table.

"Do you still lay out on the patio, or the deck, or the balcony of your house when it rains?" she asked me, turning to me on the sofa.

I looked at her, trying not to notice how big her breasts had gotten since I last saw her. Or how wide her hips had gotten. That cinched waist. Those sexy shoulders. "Y-yeah." I lost my train of thought for a minute as I glanced at how thick her thighs had gotten. Why the fuck did I drink that shit? Then it dawned on me. I hadn't had sex since the day that woman came back to town. The last time I'd had sex was when I fucked Bonnie the night before Jacyn's divorce. And that was almost three fuckin' weeks ago. I had to get out of there. The bitch was getting married, and there I was, entertaining some shit that I fucked up years ago.

I got up from the couch, only to fall right back down. I rubbed my head anxiously. "I'm drunk as fuck. I need to get home. And you gotta wake up early to marry the nigga of your dreams." I pulled my phone from my pocket. Marcellus was the only one who probably wasn't boo'd up. The only time he pulled any bitches was when his brothers were with him. If he was at the club that night, he was just watching asses jiggle. I could call him to come get a nigga.

"I was so angry at you for fuckin' my best friend." Breelyn finally brought up the subject I knew she'd bring up sooner or later, especially since we just saw the bitch at her party. "Do you know that bitch was a virgin?"

I looked at her, not sure I heard her right. I was drunk as fuck, and I assumed my eardrums were dunk as fuck, too. "Say what? Who was a virgin?"

"Delecia!" Breelyn told me.

I shook my head. "Nah, niggas told me how she got down."

"She let one boy from the basketball team play with her pussy, and he ran with it. Telling the entire team that he had sex with her! It made her popular overnight, so she ran with it. It obviously worked because it got *your* attention." Breelyn smacked her lips.

"I was young. I was just trying to forget some shit." I exhaled sharply.

"Forget what shit?" Breelyn asked.

"It doesn't even matter." I swiped up on my phone to open my contacts, so I could text bro.

"It *does* matter. Were you trying to forget me? What did I do?" Breelyn asked.

I looked at her face, and the hurt look in her eyes tugged at my fuckin' soul. "You didn't do anything, Breezy. I was going through some shit that I didn't think you would understand, so I did some shit to push you away. I was in pain, and I didn't want you to hurt with me. I made a fucked-up decision. I have never been good at processing pain. My pain always hurts other people. The last thing I wanted to do was hurt you. But, hey, at least you got the man you wanted."

Breelyn laughed out loud. "'The man I wanted'? It's been eight years since I've seen you. Science has been fuckin' other women, and that shit doesn't even bother me. And you know why it doesn't bother me?"

"I don't really care why it doesn't bother you that your nigga would rather fuck every bitch but you. That's your fucked-up business." I huffed, finding Marcellus's name in my messages. "'Nigga come get me.'" I read my text as I typed it and pressed send.

"It doesn't bother me because the only man I've ever wanted to give every piece of myself to is you!" Breelyn exclaimed.

Nigga, where? Your location is off. Marcellus texted back.

I looked up at Breelyn. "You're getting married tomorrow."

"I don't care," Breelyn told me.

I shook my head. "Don't be stupid. We're both drunk as fuck. You're supposed to be pissed at a nigga for what I did. Remember? I haven't seen you in eight fuckin' years. You're engaged to be married to a nigga that your family would want to see you with. That nigga has never been me."

"You don't miss me, Kelsius?" She ignored what I said and moved closer to me.

"You know I miss you." I couldn't even deny that shit.

She got up from the couch, teetering a little but catching her balance as she pulled that white dress over her head. She wasn't wearing anything underneath but a white thong. Those breasts sat up perfectly as if she had a built-in wire bra. Before she straddled my lap, she grabbed the smallest butt plug from the box on the table.

I chuckled nervously as I watched her slide it through her lips, licking it a little. I looked into her face as she lifted off her knees and pulled her thongs to the side to attempt to slide that plug into her asshole. I reached behind her to help her find her way since she wanted to be a big girl.

She gasped, grabbing my arm with her free hand. She shook her head frantically.

"Move your fuckin' hand, Breeze. You wanna be a big girl? You really want to take it there? Well, let's get it." I looked her in the face as she let go of my arm and moved her other hand from the butt plug. She'd gotten just the tip of it in, which was enough for me to push that muthafucka all the way inside.

Breelyn yelped out in pain, but she didn't stop me from wrapping one arm around her to pull her body into mine as I pushed the plug into her with my other hand. "Fuck, Kelsius!" she yelled. "I feel like I'm gonna shit on myself!"

I kissed her lips, chuckling. "You better not shit on me." I eyed her wedding dress hanging from the closet door in the far corner of the living room. It was wrapped in plastic, but I could see it clear as day. The wedding dress she was going to wear for a nigga who should've been me. A better version of me. The me who'd never deserve a woman like her. I wanted to back out of even fuckin' that girl that night, but then she leaned in and started sucking on my fuckin' neck. She damn near bit a nigga, sinking her teeth into my skin. And that shit felt so fuckin' good. I slid to the edge of the couch, holding her tight as I stood up. Once I made sure I had my balance, I wrapped her legs around me as I carried her toward the bedrooms, away from that fuckin' wedding dress.

"My bedroom is the last door on the left," she told me between kissing my lips.

I kissed and sucked on her lips as I made my way through her place to her bedroom. Just like the front room, everything in her room was pink as well. I sat her down on the high mattress as I kicked off my shoes and started taking off my jacket. I watched her slide out of her panties, revealing that piercing that she was talking about on that fat pussy that I'd dreamed about since we were kids. I knew that pussy would be fat and pretty. I knew she'd smell good. As soon as she opened her legs, all I smelled was sweet pheromones.

She climbed across the bed to turn on the Bluetooth speaker which was on her nightstand. "Alexa, play me some R&B love songs," she commanded, looking at me over her shoulder as she reached back and pressed the heart shaped button on her anal plug. That muthafucka started blinking purple lights. Her old favorite song by Drake, "Marvin's Room," started playing as she showed out with that arch she said she'd practiced perfecting.

She knew exactly what to do to get me to come out of my clothes. But she sat up on the bed, turning around to face me once I pulled my big black nigga out of my boxers, kicking my clothes off completely. She turned around to crawl to the edge of the bed where I stood. She sat on the edge of the bed while I opened her legs, standing between them as she pressed her thighs against my legs. She just stared at him, watching me stroke him.

"Grab him with the hand that has that nigga's rings on it." I told her, looking down at her through my drunken gaze. I let go of him, so she could grab him.

"Why's he so fuckin' big?" She gasped as she took him in both hands. "You put this big muthafucka in my friend?"

"He was about a third of this size back then. Not the same dick I had back then, baby girl. That was thirteen-year-old Kelsius.

This is twenty-one-year-old Kelsius," I told her, watching her exhale deeply as she let go of him, looking as if she was going to back out.

"I've waited my entire life for this. This night was supposed to be for my husband." She looked up at me. "*You* were supposed to be my husband."

I wasn't even sure how I was supposed to respond to that. I sat down on the bed beside her, trying to gather the right words. I wasn't good at expressing my emotions when I was sober, so I knew damn well to keep my mouth shut when I was drunk. The words would come out too harsh if I said anything with a liver soaked in alcohol.

Instead, I just sang along with Drake.

"Fuck that nigga that you love so bad. I know you still think about the times we've had..." I sang, grabbing her and pulling her onto my lap.

She turned to me, straddling my lap.

And I wrapped my arm around her waist, sliding back onto the bed until I reached her headboard. She held my face and kissed my lips.

"I waited for you, Kelsius. I wanted you to open me up first. Nobody else," she whispered.

Those words seemed to put pressure on me. Being with experienced women wasn't shit. I didn't have to teach them anything. They knew what to do and when to do it. I wasn't a fuckin' teacher. I wasn't really good with words, even when I knew exactly what she wanted to hear. That I missed her. That I loved her. That I was sorry.

"Pretty ass woman." I looked into her face as she lifted herself up a little so I could guide my dick inside her. I remembered I had condoms in my fuckin' wallet. "I have condoms in my wallet." I looked into her face.

She huffed, grabbing my dick for herself to guide it to her pussy. "Nigga, you better bark like you want this pussy and stop fuckin' playin'," she growled at me. "Do you know how long it's been since I wanted this dick? Show me what to do, and I'll do it." She panted.

I held onto her hips and pressed down as she led my dick inside of her.

The moment I felt those wet lips sliding down my dick, my entire body jerked. That shit was so slippery and wet. The warmth of that pussy was enough to make a nigga want to explode. That shit was tighter than a fist as she let him go, letting me slide up in her on my own. When she yelped out in pain, I stopped. I looked up into her face, seeing the pain written all over her face.

"I'm hurting you. I don't want to hurt you," I told her.

She opened her eyes that were clenched shut. "I-I still have the butt plug in." She pressed her breasts against my chest, so I could look behind her and see the purple light flashing between her ass cheeks. "Pull it out, please," she begged. She sat up and looked in my face as I dug in her ass to pull that muthafucka out. She squealed as I pulled it out.

"Now, show me what you saw on those videos that you watched," I said before putting the plug in my mouth and sucking that muthafucka.

Breelyn gasped in astonishment, her eyes growing bigger as I held onto her hips. And she propped herself on her feet and grabbed the top of the headboard. She didn't know what she was about to crank up. She thought she was ready to ride that muthafucka until she started to bounce and grind, and I pumped back. Not too hard but applying enough pressure to let her know I was in at muthafucka.

"It's so deep!" she squealed, slowing her pace.

"Slow down and breathe," I told her, pulling that plug from my mouth and tossing it onto the bed. I grabbed onto her hips again, eyes on her breasts as they jiggled in my face.

She shook her head frantically as she stopped pouncing and was unable to sit all the way down on it. "It's too big. Lay me on my back. And kiss me so it doesn't hurt so bad. Talk to me to put my mind on your words and not the pain," she begged me.

I held onto her as I slid down and turned over, lying her on her back and pulling her body under mine. I held her close as she wrapped her arms around me. "I wanted you to ride this dick like a fuckin' soldier," I said in her ear.

"It's too big!" she squealed as I started to grind into her. "It's so thick! Baby, it's in my fuckin' stomach! Ouuuu, you're grinding into meeee!"

"Grind back, baby. Fuck me back," I whispered to her. "Pretty baby, I know you can do it. Do it. Fuck back like you been wanting this dick inside you."

She caught my rhythm and panted as she wound her hips, matching my tempo as I dug into her. The more I ground into her, the wetter that pussy got. It started to feel like I was swimming in that pussy. I found myself having to think about other shit so I wouldn't bust all in that pussy. But then she grabbed my fuckin' dreds and started licking my fuckin' ear.

"Tell me you love this pussy." She moaned in my ear.

"Don't make me say that shit," I growled.

"Tell me you love me," she growled back.

I pulled out of her so fuckin' fast. She was not about to make me say that shit, even if that was definitely what I was feeling at the moment. I turned her over before I got off the bed. I grabbed that girl by her ankles, pulling her toward the edge, then I grabbed her by her waist. She tooted her ass up, but not enough for me. I lifted her further from the bed, pulling her ass to my pelvis as I led my dick back inside her. She tried to lose that arch, but I held her waist, pressing into the small of her back with my thumbs, massaging her back to loosen her up as I assisted in deepening her arch.

And I started stroking slowly at first. Taking those few moments to reposition helped me refocus, but she was still on that same shit as she grabbed the pink comforter, bracing herself as she started to throw it back. I watched her pussy slide up and down my dick. Her asshole was opened, too. I stuck my thumb in that muthacfucka.

She barely flinched, moaning and even looking back at me. "This shit feels just like I knew it would." She threw it back on me. "She's pretty, huh, daddy?"

"Fuck!" I tried to just focus on her ass, her pussy slobbering on my dick, and not that sexy ass voice.

"Fuck this pussy like she's yours, daddy. Beat this pussy." She threw it back on me harder. The only sound in that muthafucka was her ass clapping against me. "This dick feels so fuckin' good!" she squealed as I started digging deeper. She tried to pull away, but I pulled that muthafucka back.

"Nah, you wanted this dick. Now take him," I snarled. "Give me that muthafucka." I pounded into her, my dick growing harder with each moan she gave me. "Nut on this dick. Let that shit out. Let daddy hear that shit. Let daddy feel that shit. This is my pussy! Always been my pussy! Will always *be* my fuckin' pussy! Do you fuckin' hear me?" I grabbed her hair, wrapping it around my hand.

Her knees buckled, and she stretched out flat onto the bed.

And I followed, still drilling into her.

Though she was lying flat, that ass was still tooted up. And she still threw that ass in a circle on that dick. I slowed down to watch that muthafucka move. I wrapped my left arm around her, turning on our side a little as I smacked her ass with my right hand.

"You love me, Kelsius, don't you?" she asked me, grabbing my hand to slide it in between her legs.

I ran my fingers through her pussy lips. That shit was so fuckin' wet. "I've loved you since the first day I saw you," I finally told her.

"Then, fuck me like you love me," she cried out, and I did exactly what she said.

I pumped in and out of her until I felt her pussy pulsating around my dick. "Yeah, baby, nut on this dick. Nut all on this muthafucka."

"Daddy, cum with me." She moaned. "Cum in this pussy. Cum in your pussy, baby."

And I did. All in that pussy. I couldn't even hold back.

As soon as I busted in that pussy, I was out like a fuckin' light.

The next thing I knew, the sun was shining through the blinds on her bedroom windows. I rolled over on her bed to see that she wasn't lying next to me. I rubbed my eyes, sitting up. I had the headache from fuckin' hell. I got up, slipping into my boxers and pants. Then, I grabbed my jacket, shirt, and shoes, before heading out of the room. I walked down the hallway, making my way into the living room. There was no sign of her. I told this bitch I loved her, and she left a nigga ass-naked in her crib. I was supposed to just fuck the bitch but ended up making love by mistake.

I slipped into my shoes before it dawned on me what that day was. I looked over at the closet door where her wedding dress hung the night before. The dress was gone. She was gone. God, didn't I just ask you not to send any more stupid bitches to my life? You gonna make me strangle this bitch.

CHAPTER 10
Jacob Bobby Oxberry

"Nigga, I'ma choke this bitch!" Kelsius came barging into my house at 8:00 in the fuckin' morning.

I barely got a wink of sleep the night before because Mama had me on the phone with damn near every caterer in town, coordinating seating arrangements and practicing with the church choir to make sure everything was perfect for the wedding of the daughter of her sorority sister. Mama didn't even like Carolina but kept her close, so she could peep the competition. I don't understand women like this at all. Why keep a bitch in your circle that you didn't even like? I had enough confusion in my life, so I didn't even try to understand my mama's chaos. Then, here comes my unstable little brother, about to crash out over his baby mama. Again. Me, Jacyn, and Marcellus have been telling this nigga the type of women to avoid. But the type of women we tell him to steer clear of are the ones he crashes straight into, dick first.

"I told you to stop fuckin with Bonnie, baby boy." I laughed, rubbing my eyes before letting out a hard yawn. I plopped on the couch, watching the nigga pace back and forth. "I been told you to leave that bitch where she was weird a years ago."

"Nah, not Bonnie. Breelyn!" he yelled.

I was confused. "Breelyn? Shawty who's getting married today?" I looked at the grandfather clock, which stood in the far corner of my living room. "Who's getting married in an hour?" I looked back at the crazy nigga.

He just paced back and forth. "She made me tell her I loved her, then she went back to the nigga! I never tell these hoes I love them, and I told *her*, Jacob!"

I leaned back in the chair, watching the way my little brother started shaking. This was a part of him that he never showed to anyone but me. Jacyn's personality disorder couldn't handle the storm within Kelsius. Kelsius's pain triggered Jacyn, so Kelsius hid it from him. Marcellus didn't really care for either of them, resenting them for being in the family in the first place. And me, I was the problem solver of the family. The one who had to be calm because everyone around me was so fuckin' chaotic. I was so preoccupied with everyone else's problems that my own problems were left unattended.

"Lil bro, that girl's entire social media platform is built off the fact that she's a virgin." I watched him stop pacing back and forth, his chest continuing to heave in and out. "Or should I say *was* a virgin? Kellz, did you fuck that nigga's wife?"

"Muhfucka, she wasn't his wife when I fucked her!" Kelsius growled at me. "She said that pussy was mine!"

I laughed, picking up my coffee mug and taking a sip. "That's what they all say."

"She said she waited eight years for this dick, so I gave it to her!" Kelsius plopped down in the recliner, looking up at the ceiling.

I knew that look; he was trying to remember how many bullets he had left. And who he was going to round up with him to show up at that church.

"And you believed her?" I scoffed.

"Nigga, you just said that her social media platform is built off saving the pussy!" Kelsius yelled at me. "Why would she lie to me?"

I shrugged, taking a sip from my hot ass coffee, which was blended with just the right amount of non-dairy hazelnut creamer. "Why would she fuck you after eight years? Why wasn't she mad at you after what you did to her? Maybe she wanted something from you. I mean, you *did* fuck her friend. Maybe she was trying to pay you back. I heard Mama talking with Carolina the other night. Once Breelyn marries this nigga today, Donavan is going into partnership with Science. They'll own that casino together. Donavan is going bankrupt without Science investing into that casino. Gotta be a reason she fucked you, then said, fuck you, nigga. And I'm sure it has something to do with money or revenge. Always does."

"Yeah, whateva, nigga," Kellz muttered, then looked at me. "The fuck you about to do?"

"Drink this coffee then go meet this local R&B group, West Blvd, who's performing at the wedding." I peeped the calculated look on his face. "Why? What's up?"

"I bet she's supposed to be walking down the aisle to her favorite song, *The Secret Garden,* that song with Al B Sure!, El Debarge, and them muthafuckas." He rubbed his goatee.

I lowered my coffee cup. "And?"

"And, tell them muthafuckas they have a temporary member this morning. What color suit do I need to throw on?" Kelsius got up from the recliner, heading toward the front door.

"Lil' bro," I tried to be the voice of reason, "let this shit—"

"Yo, you gonna help a nigga? Or do I call Jacyn and his other side to help me out? He's still in the honeymoon phase. I don't wanna trigger my brother if I have to pull the trigger on this bitch on her wedding day. Now, which suit and what color tie do I need to put the fuck on?" Kelsius wasn't backing down.

* * *

There was never a point in trying to reason with Kelsius. When he had his mind set on something, I just made sure I had the car running, a lawyer on standby, and bail money if he actually got out on bail after the sick shit he had up his sleeve. Jacyn was doing well that month. No psychotic episodes since the one he had the day he found Melody on that stage at her mother's club. He'd been taking his meds. Melody would text me and Kelsius in the morning and in the afternoon when he had his doses for the day. They'd been in and out of town, traveling the past few weeks, going places she'd never been, enjoying each other. Jacyn had just gotten back in town and didn't need Kelsius fuckin' up an already hectic situation.

That Saturday morning, as soon as Kelsius left my place, I texted Jacyn to tell him that one of my college classmates wanted to buy one of his songs and wanted to meet him down at Oxberry Studios. I even made sure Melody, who had no intention of coming to her sister's wedding, would go with him. I had to keep him occupied while his brother did the fuckin' most at my parents' church.

I anxiously stood alongside the back of the church, eyeing every angle of the church. Mama went all out for her freenemie's daughter. The church was covered in purple and white lilies, matching the colors of the bridal party's clothing. West Blvd stood in front of about eight members of mama's choir, singing as the bridesmaids entered the church arm in arm with the groomsmen. Everything was going smoothly. I kept checking my watch, not to mention checking my phone. I hadn't heard from Belle in a few days.

Belle had been released from the doctor's care and had gone back home. I knew she didn't go back to the club because I made sure security text me when they saw Belle, or anyone who looked like her, entering the club. I didn't give a fuck if her car drove by the muthafucka, I wanted them to tell me that shit, too. Belle wasn't used to anyone looking after her. I was sure she thought I was too good to be true.

In the beginning, I was just doing Jacyn a favor by keeping her safe so Melody wouldn't get caught up at the club. I thought Belle was just another bitch with a troubled past who used her trauma to make excuses for the way she lived her life. But once I started talking to Belle, and really got to know her, I wanted to kiss her wounds. I didn't trauma bond with Belle; we unraveled around each other. And I needed that. So why the fuck couldn't she just call a nigga back?

Then, my phone finally chimed.

Nigga, you don't see my fuckin' texts? Scarlett's unsaved number flashed on my screen.

I hurried up and put that shit back in my pocket. You ever wish you could unfuck somebody? Yeah, she was definitely first on my list. I wasn't thinking at all the day I touched that girl. We'd gotten caught up in the moment. I'll admit, I had feelings for her growing up, but our parents had paired those two together from childhood. Scarlett wanted to make her mama happy, and Jacyn wanted to please the woman who took him and his brother in when their own family didn't. I sat back in the cut until a vulnerable moment gave me an opportunity that I should've passed up on.

As soon as the bridal party finished entering the room and took their places at the altar near the pastor and Science, the song transcended into the song that marked the entrance of the bride. Everyone stood from their seats, turning toward the church entrance to see Breelyn standing there. She looked beautiful, I'll admit. Tight, white dress that hugged her in all the right places. It had a train that trailed for at least twelve feet behind her. The cutest flower girl led her slowly down the aisle toward the altar.

Science looked so proud to see the bitch who'd just fucked my little brother last night. And she looked so happy, like she didn't let my brother unwrap the pussy that was meant for her wedding night. Everyone looked so happy, unaware that the blissful moment was definitely momentary.

I took a deep breath, feeling my brother's presence before I even looked over and saw him standing in his white suit with purple tie at the church entrance. He peeped a few of his niggas in the audience. The niggas we called to clean up the mess we were about to make. I wasn't in the fuckin' mood, man. Not over no bitch who'd fuck him, then get married the next day.

Kelsius grinned at me before placing the microphone to his lips. "I wanna read your mind, know your deepest feelings. I wanna make it right for you..." My brother had that kind of sultry voice that demanded attention. And he got the attention he wanted that morning at Oxberry Ministries.

Everyone gasped, looking in Kelsius's direction. And Breelyn froze, stopping midway down the aisle. The chorus stopped humming, the instrumental stopped playing, but my little brother kept singing his way to her.

"Here in the garden, where temptation feels so right. Passion can make you fall for what you feel. In the garden, we can make it come alive every night, oh woman... your secret garden." Kelsius sang that song like he wrote that muthafucka.

The church went deathly quiet as he approached her.

"Don't do this, Kelsius." Though Breelyn whispered, the entire church heard her. That's how quiet it was.

I stood up from leaning against the wall. Kelsius promised he wouldn't pull out his gun until he absolutely had to. The nigga was a lot of things, but he wasn't a liar. So, I trusted him for the time being.

"Ladies and gentlemen, we are gathered here today to match these two in holy matrimony." Kelsius held the microphone to his lips.

"Oh, shit..." I muttered as both Mama and Ms. Carolina stood from their seats.

"Kelsius, what are you doing?" Mama exclaimed.

"I came to ask Breelyn the same question," Kelsius answered as Breelyn turned around to face him. "I want to know how a woman can fuck someone one night, then get up and get married to another nigga."

"The fuck are you doing?" Science started to make his way down the aisle when all six of Kelsius's boys stood up one by one from their seats, from six different angles. Science stopped in his tracks at the foot of the altar.

"Why would you make me say I love you if you were still going to marry him?" Kelsius walked up to Breelyn, looking down into her face.

Breelyn was crying and frowning at the same time. "I don't know what you're talking about. Why would you come here on my wedding day and lie in the church in front of my family, his family, and yours?"

Kelsius laughed. "Y'all wanna hear a testimony today?" He pushed past Breelyn, pointing at that altar. "Pastor Lydia Oxbery's brother, Deacon Dawson Oxberry, would stand at that altar every Sunday in his Sunday best, reciting Bible verses line for line, word for word. This man that you trusted, that *I* trusted, raped me when I was nine years fuckin' old."

Loud gasps rippled across the room in waves. Mama stumbled across the people in her row to get to Kelsius, but my father jumped up to hold her back, so Kelsius could say what he needed to say out loud to everyone in our church that day.

"No amount of therapy could heal the pain that muthafucka caused me!" Kelsius yelled. "The church hid it. My adoptive parents hid it. No one talked about it. Everyone let it go for four years. Then, on our first real date to a dance, Lydia tells your aunt what happened. That shit broke me down all over again." Kelsius turned to Breelyn. "I didn't feel like a fuckin' man. The only thing I knew how to do to regain my manhood was through pussy! Thirteen-year-old me couldn't express that shit. Twenty-one year old me is man enough to admit that shit hurt! It *still* hurts!" Kelsius dried the tears I'd never seen him cry. "I hurt you because I was hurt! I'm sorry."

"Nigga, I'm sorry, too!" Science snarled, reaching into his pants. But he didn't reach fast enough.

Kelsius dug in his pants the moment he heard Science's foot hit the ground to make a move toward him. Kelsius had always been quick with the draw, gun already cocked back. The shit happened in seconds. Kelsius turned around and shot that nigga in his shoulder.

And all hell broke loose.

Muthafuckas scattered everywhere. Kelsius's niggas stayed in place, watching for anyone else with a gun. Science wasn't even known to carry. It was as if he'd expected Kelsius to show up. And where the fuck was Donovan? He missed his own daughter's wedding.

"I was trying to love you, but never mind, bitchGo put some pressure on your nigga's shoulder. He's gonna need that arm to throw that football," Kelsius growled before turning around to walk back down the aisle. He walked past me. "Turn me the fuck in, nigga."

* * *

"Why the fuck would you let my brother go to that church today?" Jacyn yelled in my face that afternoon at the Mecklenburg County police department.

"Yo. Chill out. Science pulled a gun on him first, and Kelsius defended himself. Our lawyer said this case will be dismissed once it goes to trial. We're here posting bail, bro. He's getting out. And 'let' him go to the church? I can't stop that nigga once his mind is made up, and you know that shit!" I tried to tell Jacyn, but he wasn't hearing me.

As soon as Mama ran out of the church that day, she called Jacyn to tell what I "let" the fuck happen. How the fuck was I getting blamed for what another nigga did?

"What if his crew was there with their guns and killed him? We'd be standing here having an entirely different conversation! Matter of fact, I'd be having a conversation with Mama about which suit she wanted to bury not just Kelsius in, but what suit did she want to bury *your* muthafuckin' ass in for letting this shit happen!" Jacyn shoved me in the chest.

Melody hopped up from the chair she was sitting in to get

between us. She faced Jacyn. "Baby, baby, listen to me." She grabbed his face. "Calm down."

"Where Kelsius goes, *I* fuckin' go!" Jacyn yelled. "That's *my* fuckin brother! *I'm* his fuckin' keeper, nigga, not you!" he told me.

I nodded, watching him grab Melody by the wrist and pull her off in the opposite direction. "Yeah, go get some air while we wait for them to release him," I called out.

"Nigga, fuck you!" Jacyn yelled, headed outside.

I took a deep breath, my phone chiming in my pocket. I pulled it out, frowning at the unsaved number.

We really need to talk, Jacob. Scarlett texted.

I didn't know or care what the fuck she wanted to talk about. The family had been gossiping about her lawsuit all month. I couldn't care less about the shit. Maybe that money would buy her the sense she needed to move the fuck on and stop living in her mother's shadow. Her mother was controlling her fuckin' life from the grave. She never properly grieved her mother's death, and her sisters putting the burden on her of running that company alone wasn't helping.

The phone chimed again, and I started not to even look at it when Belle's nickname, "My Woman", flashed on my phone.

I think he's been following me, Jacob... She texted.

And I went flying out of that police station.

CHAPTER 11
Jacob

"We dropped Kelsius off at home, Jacob," Melody told me over the phone as I pulled up at Belle's apartment. "His first appearance is Monday. And Science made it out of surgery."

"Fuck Science." I huffed. "Maybe sitting out for a season will put some sense into him not to pull a gun on a nigga who's got peripheral vision and hearing like a hawk. Everyone knows Kelsius's paranoid ass is quick to pull a trigger. Our lawyer will get him off."

"Y'all know this isn't over. You know how it goes down in Charlotte, celebrity or not," Melody whispered. "We have enough issues, then Kelsius pulls this. And I'm hearing you and Belle pulled up on my mother. What was that about?"

"I don't know what you're talking about." I mumbled.

"Yeah, well, I heard mama's been doing some spring cleaning at the club. Don't mess with my mama. She plays dirty. Anyway," Melody sighed, "your brother refused his meds this morning, but I put a double dose in this batter I'm about to fry this chicken in. He will be out like a light in an hour." And she hung up the phone.

It was always something with these muthafuckas. I couldn't

catch a break. Everywhere I turned, chaos. I'd worry about Kelsius when the time came. I had to see about Belle and who the fuck was following her. And why.

Messages kept popping up on my phone from Scarlett.

I was there that night those men were shot in the club. The cameras just happened to be off in the club that night, huh?

"Bitch, shut the fuck up," I said aloud as I slid my phone in my pocket and got out of my car. I hated coming to the West Side of Charlotte. I'd have to shoot a muthafucka if they side swiped my car. There was never anywhere to park at Renaissance apartments. The only time I ever came to that side of town was when Kelsius wanted to get some fuckin' weed or some E-pills for the bitches he brought home. I wished Belle would come home with me.

I knocked on her door. After a few seconds, it opened. Bonnie stood there in a fuzzy robe with matching slippers as she held the door open to let me in. She eyed my Maserati parked at the curb and shook her head. "Now why didn't you just Uber over here instead of bringing that expensive-ass car to this side of town?"

"Why are you even *on* this side of town when you should be at my place?" I responded, walking into her apartment. Even though her apartment was in the hood, the moment you walked in, you feel like you're in another world.

"Because I *have* a place, nigga." She smacked her lips, walking down her hallway.

I shut the door behind me and locked it. "I see." I walked down her hallway, admiring how spotless everything was. Her furniture was set up like a display in a showroom at an expensive furniture store. I mean, nothing was out of place. The walls and even the baseboards were clean. Candles were lit, giving the house a serene feel. It smelled like pies baking in that muthafucka. I stood in the middle of her living room, eyeing her 72-inch television hanging on her wall. "Why are you watching this sad ass shit?" I shook my head at *The Best Man Holiday* playing on the screen.

Belle rolled her eyes as she sat on her gray sectional sofa, crossing her legs and tying her robe tighter around her small waist. "It's the holidays, Jacob. I saw your family's church on the news today. And it's all over social media. They're saying that Science, that football player, was shot! What happened?"

My phone chimed in my pocket. As bad as I wanted to block Scarlett, I knew she'd just call from another number. That bitch had like eight fuckin' phones. I'd already blocked six of them.

"Long day and even longer story." I sat down beside her, loosening my tie. "Who's following you?"

Belle turned to me. "Tevin, my step father. He keeps riding up and down the street in his black F150. You can't miss that big muthafucka! Yesterday, I looked out the window to see if it was raining or not, because my WiFi was making my phone act remedial, so my weather app wasn't working. And I saw him just sitting in his car, parked right there where your car was parked. When I went outside to get the mail a few hours ago, my mailbox was empty. I look up, and he's standing alongside his car with my mail in his hands!"

I cracked my knuckles. "You want him gone?" I asked.

"I want him to stop. It's like I'm that little girl all over again. Like he wants me to take my mama's place." Belle sank back into her couch.

"Come home with me tonight. Just for tonight," I asked her. "You don't gotta pack anything. Don't even have to get dressed. Just come home."

Belle thought for a minute. "Let me grab my keys."

The moment she hit the corner of the hallway, I pulled out my phone to text my brother's plug who lived up the street to text me as soon as he saw a F150 come down Belle's street.

I could finally breathe normally after days of not hearing from Belle. Watching her walk through my house barefoot in that tank top and booty shorts felt so fuckin' good. I'd taken a shower and gotten out of the clothes from the wedding. It was around dinner, the perfect time to cook for her, to remind her of the food I'd made for her while she stayed with me in the mountains.

"Never met a man whose cooking makes me feel like I'm in a five-star restaurant at home." Belle smiled at her plate as soon as I set it in front of her. "I love salmon!"

I laughed at her pronunciation of the word.

Belle frowned at me, blending her veggies with her brown rice in her place as she sat across from me at the table in my kitchen nook. "What?"

"Theres' no 'l' in 'salmon.'" I told her, cutting into my medium steak.

"Umm, yes, there is. The word is literally spelled s-a-*l*-m-o-n." She spelled the word out to me like a nigga didn't know how to spell what I just cooked for her.

"Yeah, but it's pronounced SAM-un. The 'l' is silent." I grinned at her.

Belle rolled her big, pretty eyes. "Like *you* need to be silent?"

I laughed out loud, watching her grin a little as she ate some of her food before taking a sip of her favorite wine. Takura Japanese Plum Wine. When she stayed with me, she'd mentioned to me that her favorite food was Japanese food, and her favorite wine was Takura Japanese Plum Wine. I made sure that when she was well enough to drink again, I kept it stocked in my fridge. I tried it out for myself, not thinking I'd like cheap ass wine, but the shit wasn't bad. Tastes like apple juice, and after two or three glasses of that shit, you start floating like a muthafucka.

"Pretty ass." I watched her eat. "I missed you."

Belle pursed her lips. "I don't need you babysitting me the way that you do your family. I'm a big girl. Yeah, I got scared when I saw my stepfather creeping around, but I'm good now. I haven't gone back to the club. I'm actually trying out for some dance auditions. Maybe get a job at the mall for the holidays."

"We could use a secretary down at the recording studio. I could use a personal assistant," I told her, watching her eat.

"You can ask one of your hoes to make copies and answer the phone." Belle scoffed.

I frowned. "What hoes?"

"The hoes y'all fuck in VIP every weekend. Don't fuckin' play with me." Belle rolled her eyes, forcefully digging into her plate.

"You have a nigga confused with my brothers. I haven't had sex in a minute, mamas," I admitted.

"When was the last time?" She pursed her lips.

I dreaded thinking about it. "Before my brother's wedding." That was all she needed to know. "Damn near three months ago. Back in August or some shit. I go to the strip club for the dances. For the fantasy. The strip club took my mind off thinking about a woman who I had no business thinking about, much less fuckin'. The strippers at that club are the complete opposite of everything that woman represented, and I needed that."

Belle looked at me, a mix between curiosity and hurt on her face. "Do you still love her?"

I shook my head. "Nah. Was never supposed to love her."

"A man like you, you're supposed to be in love." She looked around the breakfast nook then off into the kitchen. "Educated. Cultured. Well-traveled. Articulate. Business savvy. Well groomed. Best dressed. Musically inclined. Not too bad to look at either." She rolled her eyes playfully before getting up from the table, carrying her plate with her.

"You're full already?" I asked, watching her go over to where I had a few Tupperware stacked.

"Kinda wanna hear some music, drink a little. I can eat this later if I get hungry," she answered, scraping her food into a Tupperware.

I got up from the table and walked into the kitchen, watching her place her plate into the sink. She took my plate from my hands, storing my food away as well. When I attempted to wash the dishes, she grabbed my hand, telling me she'd do them. So, I let her. And I grabbed the bottle of wine and headed toward my living room to turn on my 96-inch TV, which was mounted above my fireplace. And I turned on YouTube, something I saw her do the two weeks she was staying with me. I buried myself in my work while we stayed in the mountains to keep myself from putting my hands all over her. She needed comfort, not my fuckin' hormones. When I would check in on her, she was either exercising along with videos on YouTube or watching '90s videos.

"On a perfect day, I know that I can count on you..." Johnny Gill sang through the television speaker.

"Uh-oh, the '80s and '90s crash out songs." Belle giggled. "We had those niggas ready to crash out in them R&B songs! Wanya in *Bended Knee*, swallowing his pride, saying he was sorry, stop pointing fingers, the blame was on him! Shit, Jodeci was asking bitches to just stay for a little while. Don't get me started on Keith Sweat's begging ass."

I laughed out loud. "My dad would wait until Mom went to choir practice to throw on some Keith Sweat or R. Kelly." I watched her walk into the living room. "You gonna dance with me?"

Belle smiled shyly as she walked up to me.

"Through the good times and bad times, she will always," I sang along with the music, "always be right there." I grabbed her by her waist, pulling her closer to me.

"Do you think..." Belle stopped as she slid her arms over my shoulders. "Never mind. It's stupid."

I shook my head. "Nah, say it." I looked down at her as we swayed to the music.

"Do you think someday I will have what Melody has with Jacyn? Have you seen them together?" Belle smiled at the thought. "She's the beauty, and he's like this tamed beast. I think she tames him."

I couldn't deny it. "She's part of what tames the beast in him, yeah, I will admit that."

"Their love happened by accident." Belle's smile faded before she looked back at me looking at her admirably.

I disagreed. "Nothing that happens is by accident. Everything has a purpose. Even this moment right now. It was already designed. It was mapped out before it even happened."

"So, my love life is planned out?" she asked me, and I nodded. "Is this a part of it? Are *you* are part of it?"

"I could be," I told her.

"But do you want to be?" she asked.

I couldn't even deny my attraction for her. "I wanna be, yeah."

"Why?" she asked as if she wasn't expecting me to answer.

"I just want to be with you. It's as simple and as complicated as that, if that makes sense." I started to explain. "I must've checked my phone a thousand times within the past few days, looking for your text or missed call. I missed having you near me those two weeks. I loved planning, providing, protecting and surprising you with little things. When I could sense that you were off, I wanted to fix whatever was wrong. When I wasn't in the best mood those days, you stayed with me. Hearing your laughter even when you were in another room brightened my entire day. That night you laid beside me on the balcony, and we let the rain hit us in the face, I've never felt more at peace." I grabbed her hand and held it to my chest. "Now, dancing with you in the middle of my living room calms me down. You don't know the day I've had. Shit, you don't know the life I'd had these past twenty-three years. This right here feels good. This simple shit is much needed."

"Even from a Midnight Ballerina?" Belle's voice softened to a whisper. "I'm far from innocent. I've done some bad things."

I agreed. "I've done some things that I'm carrying with me today. Things I can't escape. Things that will hurt a lot of people. Things I can't take back." I backed into my chaise, sitting down on it and pulling her down with me.

Belle turned to me, throwing her left leg over my lap and scooting her body into mine so her breasts were pressing against me. And she kissed my lips. "Well, then, I guess we've both been bad." She giggled as I held her hips and scooted all the way back on the chaise.

I leaned back as she sat directly on it. My dick got hard in my lounge pants as soon as she started winding her hips. The dick wasn't even inside her yet, and she was hunchin' that muthafucka.

"Got *damn*," I said.

"My body count resets with you, right?" Belle asked and I nodded.

"Hell yeah," I told her, watching her reach for the drawstring to my pants. I grabbed her hand. "Whoa," I chuckled a little, "what you doing?"

"Sucking that long, stressful day out of you. I've never done this before, remember? I want to give it a try." She told me, pushing my hand out of the way.

My shit started throbbing the moment I felt her fingertips in my pants. Then, she grabbed it and pulled it out of my pants. I lifted up from the chair, so I could pull my pants further down, but she pulled the muthafuckas down for me. She took one look at my dick before kissing me, then kissing him.

I looked down at her, biting my lip at the sight of drool sliding from the corners of her lips before she even started sucking. Then, she licked the tip like she was licking a Blo-Pop. I moaned and immediately grabbed a fist full of thick hair as she pulled my dick into her throat with my tongue.

My toes immediately balled up. She pulled my dick past her tonsils, her tongue sliding right between my fuckin' balls. It took everything in me not to scream out like a little ass girl. And then she pushed my dick in and out of her mouth, just using her throat muscles.

"Shit, slow down..." I hissed, fisting her hair. "Open your eyes and look at what you're doing to me. Slow down and look up at me."

Belle opened her eyes, looking up at me. And just as she started flicking her tongue on my dick, the doorbell rang. She let my dick plop out of her mouth before sitting up from the chair.

I wasn't expecting company. I got up from the chair, pulling up my pants and tucking my dick inside, trying to make him go down. I dug in my pants pocket for my phone. The only text I'd gotten was from the plug, telling me that Tevin had driven by Belle's place twice and asking if I wanted him to trail the next time that he saw him. Just when I started to text the nigga back, the doorbell rang again.

"So, you're really not gonna answer my fuckin' calls, Jacob?" Scarlett shouted from the other side of the door.

Belle squinted at me in disbelief. "I know that's not fuckin' Scarlett. Why the fuck is she at your door? Answer it so I can slide this bitch for Melody tonight." Belle immediately took off the hairband she had around her wrist and started tying her hair up. "Ouuu, I've been waiting for this shit. Open the door."

"*Fuck,*" I muttered, walking toward the front door.

I'd been ignoring the bitch purposely for weeks. She was stalking my brother, following him to Greece. Getting my mother to go with her to her prenatal visits. Having her nosy ass sisters driving by the building where Jacyn's new practice was about to open. She was doing the fuckin' most over a dead situation. And since she couldn't fuck with him, she was there to fuck with me.

I answered the front door. I barely pulled the muthafucka open when she pushed her way through. I started to sling the bitch right out the door, but she pulled away from me, pushing me out of the way so she could walk past me. She giggled a little at the sight of Belle making her way toward the front door.

"Ms. Lydia said that you were keeping Melody's pet, but I didn't believe her." Scarlett laughed.

"Well, Melody's pet bites, bitch." Belle approached us.

I turned to Belle. "Babe, please, go have a seat."

Belle looked behind her at the bench in my hallway. She wasn't leaving my side apparently. She was already removing her earrings as she sat down on the bench and folded her arms.

Scarlett rolled her eyes. "Kelsius isn't going to get out of this bullshit he got himself into today. One of Breelyn's cousins was at the club that night. She said she was going to testify that Kelsius is violent and that he shot a nigga in the club a few weeks ago."

"White bitches saying 'nigga' is crazy." Belle scoffed.

"I'm about as white as that baby you gave up for adoption last year," Scarlett hissed.

Belle got up from the bench. "What did you say?"

That was just like Scarlett to go digging up dirt on anyone she felt threatened by. I was sure the moment she found out that me and Belle were witnesses at Jacyn's wedding that day, she'd gone digging up dirt on Belle. Any woman who got near me, Scarlett had an issue. The bitch wanted her Jacyn and her Jacob, too.

"Your Stage Sisters do a lot of talking when they feel like you've abandoned them." Scarlett smirked. "They say you told Melody that your baby died at birth, wouldn't even let her come see you deliver the baby at the hospital. You told your best friend that the baby died, when you left that baby in the nursery and never went back. The woman who adopted your baby just lost her husband a month ago. She can't afford her mortgage. That baby is going right back into the system. When I win this lawsuit, maybe I'll open an orphanage. I'll make sure she's taken care of."

Belle immediately tried to run straight at Scarlett's neck, but I blocked her path. "Jacob, I will beat that fuckin' baby out of her, I promise you!"

I slung Belle out of the way before turning to Scarlett. "Yo, why the fuck are you here? Kelsius has a lawyer to defend him. Belle's business is none of *your* fuckin' business. And Joel is with my mama's family today. Jacyn is picking him up in the morning."

Scarlett nodded. "Okay, sounds good." She eyed Belle sitting back down on the bench behind me. "It's funny she should mention babies. I'm a high-risk pregnancy, so they offered to do an amniocentesis on me since I'm fourteen weeks pregnant."

The family always depended on me when it came to accounting or keeping the books straight because I could calculate large numbers in my head without a calculator. The moment she mentioned fourteen weeks, I started adding shit up. Scarlette told my brother that the baby was conceived the night she told him it was over. August 28th. It was now November 21st. If she conceived the baby on August 28th, that would make her twelve weeks pregnant and not fourteen. My heart started pounding in my chest.

"Get the fuck out of my house," I told her.

"I thought I was twelve weeks pregnant," she went on to say, "but the doctor said I had the amount of amniotic fluid of a person between fourteen and sixteen weeks pregnant. So, she ran some tests. They tested the DNA to check for birth defects and genetic disorders. Fortunately, they didn't find any. Instead, the tests confirm that Joel and the baby girl that we're having share the same father."

Everything got so quiet. The only noise in the house was the humming from the refrigerator. It didn't take long for Belle to realize what was going on.

"She's the married woman, huh?" Belle laughed a little, getting up from the bench. "Nigga, Joel is *your* son? He's the baby you have out there? Now you're having *another* baby with this bitch?"

Fuck...

Also by Krystal Armstead

A Single Virgin: An Arrange Marriage
I Picked The Wrong N!gga 3
I Picked The Wrong N!gga 2
I Picked The Wrong N!gga
Knocked Up By My Millionaire Crush 3
Knocked Up By My Millionaire Crush 2
Knocked Up By My Millionaire Crush
Saved By The Millionaire Next Door 3
Saved By The Millionaire Next Door 2
Saved By The Millionaire Next Door
I Let A Country Boy Get Me Pregnant 3
I Let A Country Boy Get Me Pregnant 2
I Let A Country Boy Get Me Pregnant
A Single Woman & The Thug Next Door 3
A Single Woman & The Thug Next Door 2
A Single Woman & The Thug Next Door
When They See Us Together 2
When They See Us Together
On Every Thug I Love

www.ingramcontent.com/pod-product-compliance
Lightning Source LLC
Chambersburg PA
CBHW022036220526
45357CB00059B/276